LIFE IN A
SMALL TOWN

PALMETTO
P U B L I S H I N G
Charleston, SC
www.PalmettoPublishing.com

Paperback ISBN: 979-8-8229-4483-1
eBook ISBN: 979-8-8229-5495-3

LIFE IN A
SMALL TOWN

Lana Shevlin

DEDICATION

———————

I would like to dedicate this book to my parents,
Tom and Betty McCart. They have both passed, but they gave me the
best childhood ever. They were hard-working and loving parents who
made a modest income. They made me feel like I could achieve my
dreams if I worked for them.

To my son Ronnie, who died at the age of twenty-six,
who left a hole in my heart, that can never be filled.

To my only sibling, my brother Tommy Kelly
who died of ALS at the age of fifty-seven.

To my husband Bob, who has put up with me for forty-three years
and is the love of my life.

I will forever be grateful for all that they have taught me.

———⫽———

PROLOGUE

As you look around the town of Bradleyville, it looks like your typical small-town Americana. The streets are lined with dogwood and oak trees. In the town square is the elementary school that was built in 1922. There's a bandstand where weekend concerts are still played. Under the bandstand is the police department. Some of my greatest memories as a child were on the playground where the carnival is held every year.

We used to gather in the afternoons and watch the jocks play and perform on the basketball court. The stores that surround the square have changed over the course of time. The movie theater is the type with a balcony where you can go on a date and feel isolated from the outside world. There's still a dime store, although you'd have a hard time finding anything that actually costs a dime.

What would any small town be without its local hangout? In Bradleyville, the local hangout is Herley's. Herley's is the kind of place that holds memories for several generations, memories of going after school with your friends and talking for hours while having a nickel box of pretzels and a nickel bottled coke. The people you pass on the street have known you all your life and greet you by name and ask how your family is.

Bradleyville looks serene; that's why it is so hard to believe that everything that happened over the last year and a half really happened.

A longtime prominent resident turned out to be involved in multiple crimes, and for a short time, a murderer lived among the locals and was treated with kindness. Does this make the residents too-trusting country bumpkins?

When you grow up in a town like Bradleyville, you not only grow up with the love and support of your family, but the entire town looks out for you. Of course, the drawback is the entire town also knows what you have done pretty much before you've done it. People don't feel the need to lock their doors. You know your neighbors by name, and you know them because they have helped you at some time of need, as you have helped them. They celebrate your happy times and comfort you during the bad times.

One such family is the Prackets: Ida, Bob, Dawn, and Whitney. They live on a working farm just outside of town. The land has been in the Pracket family for six generations.

—⫻—

CHAPTER ONE

D awn had lived in Bradleyville all her life. She had never regretted missing the big cities. She loved the simple country life and the familiar faces.

She had had a terrific time growing up. School had been filled with activities and friends she had known since she was a baby. She was a true animal lover, her favorite being her horse, Queenie.

Her mother had been so proud when she had gotten accepted at some of the top colleges in the States. She had tried to get her to at least go look at some of them.

She, of course, had offered to go with her and tour the campuses but to no avail.

Dawn told her, "Mama, I just want to go to Orange County Junior College and so does Donna. We are gonna be roommates. It is only three hundred and fifty miles from home, so if I get homesick, I can come back for a visit."

Dawn just did not have the need to break away like a lot of young people do after graduation. Ida was disappointed, but she wanted her daughter to be happy.

She was scared when Dawn decided to wait a year before going to college. She was sure her daughter would decide to forgo leaving her secure home to see and experience anything new.

But the day finally came for Dawn to leave for college.

As she watched her daughter pack her car, she thought of all the dreams she had for her. She had thought Dawn was destined for important things, a real career. Something Ida had wanted for herself. That and travel. She looked at her beautiful daughter and thought how very much she was like her father.

Bob Pracket was born and raised in Bradleyville. Generations of Prackets had been content to live here and die here. Bob's philosophy was "When you have everything you need or want nestled right here in the middle of this heavenly country, why would you want to leave?" This had been a cause of disagreement between Ida and Bob for the better part of their marriage. Of course, Ida had given up on getting out of Bradleyville years ago, but she had hopes for her daughters.

Dawn and Whitney were giggling as they walked together to the car. They had a unique relationship as sisters: they were best friends. Dawn was only nine months older than Whitney. Neither one of them could remember life without the other one being part of it. They used to tell people they were twins, but Whitney, who always liked to sleep in, just was not ready to come out. She needed to keep hitting that nine-month snooze alarm.

They even looked alike except for their coloring. Dawn had blond hair and blue eyes, and Whitney had black hair and green eyes. They were built alike, both around five foot four and slender—not skinny. Just right.

They were quite different as far as their personalities were concerned. Dawn was more serious, quiet, and sweet. Whitney was outspoken and not afraid of anything.

Dawn looked at her sister and said "I'm gonna miss you, sis. Who am I gonna tell all my deep, dark secrets to?"

Then they both half laughed, half cried.

Not much was a secret in Bradleyville. Heck, everybody in town knew everybody else's business.

"I'll be home for Thanksgiving, and you can visit me and Donna. It is not that far away, you know," Dawn said.

With tears in their eyes, they hugged one last time.

"Mom, what am I gonna do without your home cooking?"

Ida Pracket stood with tears in her eyes and hugged her daughter and told her to take care of herself and to enjoy being someplace new. "Don't you forget to take plenty of pictures and send them to me." With this came the hardest part, telling her daddy goodbye.

She looked at him, and he looked so sad. She could tell he thought he was losing his little girl. At that moment, she almost decided not to go. She was so happy right here with her family and friends. It was comfortable.

Ida could sense her wavering, so she spoke up. "You had better get a move on it. I do not want you driving too fast or being on the highway at night alone."

Dawn came back to reality. She knew she had to get going now or she would never leave.

"Bye, daddy. I will be home before you know it." She hugged this man who had taught her to fish, swim, ride a horse, and treat animals with respect. He had always been there for both of his daughters. He thought they were darn near perfect. She would miss him so much. She got in her car, let the windows down to wave one last goodbye, and then turned and drove away from her home and her security. She glanced once more to see her dad and sister hugging each other and her mom waving. Then she did not look back.

———#———

Dawn finally turned on the radio to get her mind off the ache in her heart, singing and looking around as she drove from familiar places into the unknown. This was uncharted territory. She had to admit she was getting a little excited. There were so many new things ahead of her; new people, a new school, and her old-time friend, Donna.

Donna had gone up a little over two weeks ago and had been shopping for everything she said they needed to make it into the kind of place they had always dreamed of having as girls. Dawn, Whitney, and Donna had been like the three musketeers as long as they could remember.

Donna had dated more than Dawn throughout school. She always teased Dawn about ending up with a horse instead of a husband. She had her share of invitations; she just did not seem to have time for dating. She would much rather go out with a group of friends. Besides, she had known all the boys around Bradleyville since they had been babies together. She enjoyed their company, but they seemed more like brothers than boyfriends. She did dream one day of getting married to a terrific man and raising a family together in Bradleyville. She wanted an old farmhouse that they could renovate together, and there had to be animals and horses, of course. She wanted four children, and she wanted to stay home with them and be a typical farm homemaker. The only problem was she had not met the father of those imaginary children yet. She knew when she did finally meet her future husband that everything would explode in her heart.

—*//*—

Whitney, on the other hand, had a date with a different boy every weekend. She was extremely popular and outgoing. She knew just what she wanted to do when she finished school. She was going to be a journalist—and not just on the hometown paper either. She wanted to travel to all areas of the country and especially outside the United States.

In fact, she had been taking college courses at night for a couple of years now, and she had a part-time job on the *Bradleyville Times*. Her boss had worked with a famous international journalist, Mary Whitman. Mary had been one of the first women editors, and she had been helping her friend with the paper while she took a little R & R in Bradleyville. She had taken Whitney on as her protégé. She was the most interesting person Whitney had ever met.

Mary had been to every country imaginable, and she had won more than her share of literary awards for excellence in journalism. Whitney was totally in awe of her.

I guess Mom will get her wish one day with at least one of her daughters. Whitney fully intended to travel the globe.

CHAPTER TWO

———————

Dawn had been driving for about four hours and decided it was time for a break and some gas. Her car was not a brand-new one, but she loved it and really appreciated her parents sacrificing what she knew they really could not afford so she could have it. It was a Volkswagen Beetle with a new paint job, brand-new interior, and, at her dad's insistence, new tires and brakes. It was baby blue with black leather seats and a gray interior. She had always wanted one ever since she saw her first *Love Bug* movie. She just never grew out of it.

Let's see, there is a nice-looking little diner and a gas station right up ahead. Perfect. I can use some coffee and a bite to eat, Dawn thought.

As she pulled away from the gas station and into the diner parking area, she noticed the man in the car parked next to her. He had black silky hair, mahogany brown eyes, and a body to die for.

She looked away when he turned to get a better look at her. He got out of his car and smiled as he walked by and into the diner. He was about six feet tall.

Whoa, girl. What a smile, she thought.

He had been driving a candy-apple red Corvette with a camel interior. It was an older model but in showroom condition, and so was he. She blushed as she thought about the effect he had had on her, just from a smile. She checked her hair and lip gloss before getting out of the car and seeing him again.

The diner was typical of all little country diners. It had a jukebox playing and some of the locals sitting around passing the time. On the counter were stacked containers with the most delicious-looking homemade pies inside. It made her think of her mama's delicious pies and cakes. Her weakness was coconut cream pie. She had already decided if they had coconut cream pie that it would be lunch—that and coffee. After all, there was no one around to scold her for not eating a proper meal. She took a seat in one of the booths so she could look out the window, but her eyes just kept straying over to the counter where that good-looking guy sat.

"Hey, it's okay to lust a little in your mind," she thought. As a matter of fact, it is healthy.

In no time at all, a girl about her age in jeans and a western shirt came over to take her order. To Dawn's delight, they had fresh coconut pie. The waitress brought her a huge slice and a piping hot cup of coffee.

"Hi there. My name is Patsey Conners. Are you from around here? I have never seen you in here before and eventually everybody comes in." She was so bubbly that Dawn was at once at ease with her.

"No, I live in Bradleyville. I am on my way to Monroe. I am going to be going to Orange County Junior College."

At this, Patsey proceeded to just plop right down in the seat across from Dawn. "No kidding! I'm going to OCJC too. We can get together while we are there. None of my friends are going there, so it would be nice to have a friend to get together with."

The man's voice came from the counter. "Pats, do you think you might be able to get me some more coffee before I choke on your meat-loaf?" He said it with a smile and an air of familiarity.

Patsey knows this gorgeous guy? Dawn wondered. Patsey rolled her eyes at the man's comment and said, "yeah, yeah, hold on to your britches, I'm coming. A person cannot even take a break in this place."

While Patsey was up, she went down the counter filling coffee and chatting with the customers. Patsey was so easygoing and fun-spirited. It would be fun getting to know her at school. She had shoulder-length auburn hair and smiling brown eyes. She was not exactly pretty—more like the girl next door. She was Dawn's size. Dawn could already imagine them trading outfits at school. Dawn, Whitney, and Donna had always traded clothes, sometimes they forgot which outfit belonged to who.

Donna had the most expensive labels since her father was the richest man in Bradleyville. He was a lawyer and owned his own firm. You could not really call their house a house; it was more like a mansion. Frank MacIntosh owned a lot of real estate in and around Bradleyville. People used to joke around that the bank went to him to borrow money. He had raised Donna on his own since she was almost three years old. Dawn and Whitney did not spend much time at Donna's since her dad was stiff. Donna seemed to thrive at the Pracket house. She loved being there. She really missed not having a mother, so Ida tried to be there for her like she was her own daughter.

Mom had known Donna's mother a long time ago. She did not really know her as a friend, just as someone who lived in the neighborhood. She said her mom had been a bit of a wonderer, or it seemed that way. She had taken off once about four years before Donna was born and stayed away for two years. She said the talk around town was that everyone thought Frank MacIntosh was crazy when he took her back. The next and last time she left, he filed for divorce and full custody of Donna. No one had really known Mrs. MacIntosh. She rarely came out of the house. Whenever you would see her out in the gardens, she looked so sad and alone. Ida had always felt bad that she had not tried harder to be a friend. Then she moved on without her daughter. It was upsetting for Mom to think of a mother leaving her child. There was, without a doubt, more to the story!

Donna barely remembered her mom, but she never stopped hoping to see her again. Her dad had told her he would try to find her if Donna wanted him to.

He made sure to apply the right amount of guilt by letting Donna know how much he had been hurt when his wife left, and he said he certainly hoped that Donna wouldn't get hurt if she ever did find her mother. Well, after that Donna never brought it up to her dad again. He had tried to shield Donna from the pain and heartache of not having a mother in the typical male way: he bought her everything she wanted.

All things considered; Donna was not a spoiled brat. She was generous and would give you the shirt off her back if she thought you needed it. She volunteered at the hospital and even went down to the local library every Thursday evening, where she sat and read stories to a group of kids. Donna loved kids, and when one of her kids saw her on the street or at church, they would run up to her and hug her and say, "Hi, Miss Donna. See ya Thursday." Donna would glow. I guess it is not surprising that she was taking courses to be a teacher in college. Although the only real reason either she or Donna were going to college was because it was expected of them and, of course, to meet that perfect guy. That is a contradiction of terms ("perfect" and "guy"). Oh well you can hope. Marriage and children were all they really wanted.

I must have been in my own little world when Patsey finally came back to my booth. I do not even remember her sitting down, but there she was, sitting and smiling at me as though she was giving me time to come too.

"Welcome back," she said. We laughed.

"I do not know where my mind was. This is my first time to be away from home totally on my own. I am going back over my whole life and daydreaming a lot."

Out of the kitchen came a couple. They were a little older than my parents. Both had white aprons, and they were holding hands, which I thought was so sweet.

Patsey introduced us., Wilma and Jake Collins, this is Dawn, and she is headed for OCJC too. I think we're going to be friends."

They came over smiling as if they had known me all my life. We chatted for a while, and then Jake, Patsey's dad, called over to the counter, "Jimmy, now you've got two young women to watch out for at school."

For a while, I could not breathe. He was talking to that hunk, I had been trying not to stare at him.

Jimmy. So that was his name. He could watch over me any time he wanted to. This was ridiculous, I didn't even know this person. I have never felt like this over a boy, but then this was no boy—he was all man.

When he got up and started walking toward my booth, my stomach knotted up. I hoped I could speak with some semblance of intelligence if he spoke to me.

"Hi, I am Jimmy McCoy. I see you know my little cousin. She has never told me about you."

"That's because I just met her when I came in to eat. I'm Dawn Pracket. We discovered that we are both going to Orange County Junior College."

I guess I will have my hands full then." Jimmy sighed.

"What are you talking about?" Dawn replied.

"I'll have my hands full keeping an eye on the two of you." Jimmy responded.

"Are you going there too?" Dawn asked

"I'm an instructor hoping to get a government grant in agriculture," he said.

"That sounds interesting," she said.

"Sure, it does. Isn't that what people say when they are too bored to say anything else?"

Jimmy taunted.

"I don't know what most people do, but I'm not that rude." she said sharply.

He looked right into my eyes as if he could see down to my soul, and with a cocky grin on his face, he turned to Patsey and told her not to be late when he picked her up in the morning because he had a staff meeting. He smiled and exchanged a few words with Patsey's parents and walked to the door. He turned and told her, "It was nice meeting you, Dawn Pracket."

Dawn watched as he got into his Corvette and drove away. Jake and Wilma had gone back into the kitchen and Patsey was talking to her, but she had not heard a word.

"Sorry, I zoned out for a few minutes. What were you saying?"

"Would you like to get to know him better?"

I just rolled my eyes in that "yeah, right" look.

The girls started talking about where they were going to be living, and Dawn found out Patsey would be bunking with Jimmy until she found a place. She had been looking but so far had not found anything she could afford.

"Well, I might know of a place." Patsey was at once interested. "My roommate, Donna, and I are looking for someone to share expenses with. We really do not pay rent, just utilities and groceries."

"Why don't you pay rent?"

"Donna's dad owns the house, and he arranged for us to live there while we are in school. Of course, Donna would have to agree, but I just know the two of you will get along just fine let me give you my cell number and address, and when you get there give me a call. You can come over and meet Donna. You can look things over and see what you think. We can settle all the details after the two of you meet."

Patsey ran off to the kitchen to tell her parents about finding a place to live, and from the sounds coming from the kitchen, they were as excited as Patsey about finding a place for their daughter to live.

"I need to be going. Donna is expecting me, and I had only meant to stop for a quick bite to eat."

We made plans to get together the next day, and I headed off for the last half of the trip. I really did like Patsey, but to be honest, there was a bonus in having her as a roommate. I got to know Jimmy better. I did not know what it was about him. I just felt drawn to him. He was sexy. What was I thinking? He probably already had a girlfriend and would not be interested in a small-town girl like her anyway. Oh well. A girl could dream.

CHAPTER THREE

———————

The time flew, and before she knew it, she was pulling into the driveway of what was to be her new home. The house was a large three-story Victorian. It needed some paint, but other than that, it was beautiful. There were wraparound porches that traveled the whole circumference of the house. There were balconies on both the second and third floors, a detached garage, and even a small cottage out back that I suppose was a servants' quarters at one time. There were beautiful flowers and shrubs that were being taken over by weeds. There was even a rose garden with a gazebo in the center. You could hardly see it for all the vines. All things considered; it was perfect.

I could not wait to see the inside. As she walked up the steps to the front door, she noticed a note stuck to it.

Hi girl,

I had to pick up some groceries. I will not be long. Use the key I sent you and have fun looking around. You'll know which bedroom is yours when you see it. I know your taste in decorating, but don't worry. You can change anything you want. I'll only pout for a few minutes, I promise.

Love 'n stuff,
Donna

Dawn was pleased to have this time alone to get to know this beautiful old house. The sign that hung on the side of the front door was pure Donna.

Welcome to our humble home
If we are not friends when you arrive
Our desire is that we will be by the time you leave

I loved it. She opened the door and inside were hooks to hang coats on and an umbrella stand. The room to the right was small but quaint. It is what used to be called a parlor. It had a double-faced fireplace; one side opened into the parlor, and the other side opened into the living room. The furniture in the parlor was covered in a country floral pattern. There was a settee, two chairs, and a small coffee table topped with a doily that hung over the sides. In the center was a gorgeous bowl filled with blush-pink roses. In one corner was an antique spinning wheel.

There was an old-fashioned floor lamp, and on the wall hung a painting of a field of flowers with a lady sitting against an oak tree. Across from the parlor was the library. Every wall was lined with bookshelves from the ceiling to the floor, and the only furniture was a plain old table with four ladder-back chairs. There was a reading lamp on the table, and that was it. There was a short hall and then a big country kitchen. It was light and simple but comfortable and inviting. From the sink, you could see the whole backyard and hear the birds singing in the trees. I thought I am gonna like it here.

There was a large walk-in pantry with stairs leading down to the basement. The basement was huge. In the laundry area, there was a corner set up for sewing, which Donna knew I would love. It had an old treadle sewing machine that had been converted to electric. There was also a corner with a potting table and all the gardening equipment anyone would need. By the looks of the yard, these would get used a lot. I couldn't wait to see the rest. So far, this house was amazing. It was as if Donna took notes all those years when we were playing house.

Across from the kitchen was the living room. All the furniture was strategically placed around the fireplace so anyone sitting could take full advantage of both the heat and ambiance. Somehow, I knew there would be a piano, but I never dreamed it would be an old-time player piano. In a big basket beside the piano were about twenty extra rolls of music. I closed my eyes and could imagine someone sitting at the piano. I could hear laughter and singing. There were friends sitting on the overstuffed couch talking, and a glow coming from the fireplace. It felt so warm and comfortable. This was indeed the kind of home we had dreamed of. I nearly jumped out of my skin when Donna came bounding into the room. I had not even heard her open the door or go into the kitchen with the groceries.

"Well, what do you think?"

The smile on my face let her know how pleased I was. "I can't believe you've done all this by yourself. It's amazing."

We hugged and both started talking at once. "Have you seen your bedroom yet?"

"No, I have been exploring the first floor, and I got caught up daydreaming."

Then we hugged each other hello again.

"Go on up. I want to see your face when you see your bedroom."

"Well, now my curiosity is piqued."

Donna was half shoving Dawn up the stairs.

"Okay, I am going."

I got to the second floor, and Donna motioned me on up. "Keep going, Rapunzel. You're on the third floor."

"But I want to see it all."

"You will in time. I have been waiting all day for you to get here, and I cannot wait any longer."

She made me close my eyes while she opened my door. When I looked, I just stood there with my mouth open. I could not speak. She had completely duplicated my room from home, right down to my favorite stuffed animals and even the pictures on the wall. My eyes started to tear up.

"How on earth did you manage to do this?"

"Believe me, it was not easy. Whitney was a big help. I can't believe she managed to keep it a secret. She got copies of pictures and pieces of fabric. She took pictures of your room and sent them to me. The hard part was getting your personal things here before you got here."

"Yeah, how did you do that?"

"Ms. Whitman was coming this way on her way to Atlanta, so Whitney boxed them up yesterday and Mary dropped them off last night. She mentioned that Whitney was going to be graduating early and going to work for her full time."

"I wondered why she insisted on helping me so much with my packing and asked me to stay in her room last night so we could talk all night. That little minx."

"Well, I knew how much you dreaded leaving home, and I wanted to make it as easy as I could. I didn't want you getting homesick and taking off on me halfway through the semester. Oh, I almost forgot. Go open your French doors."

I did as commanded. It was a balcony that overlooked the area of the backyard where the gazebo was. There was a rocker and a small table on it.

"I thought on clear nights you could sit out here and read, or daydream, or just escape my chatter for a while."

I was trying to take it all in when she whisked me away again. "I couldn't duplicate your bathroom, but I think you'll approve. It's over there." Donna pointed across the hall.

"It's spectacular and so big." I wondered where the closet was. "I have always wanted a dressing room and vanity, but you knew that didn't you?"

Donna, looking as proud of herself as could be, just stood there smiling. "Come on. I have a room too, you know." She grabbed my hand,

and down we went to the second floor. There were two bedrooms, each with their own bathroom. In the hall was a large linen closet.

Donna's room was a vision of spring colors. She had a canopy bed, and on her windows were white priscilla curtains. There was one of those long lounging chairs with fancy little pillows on it. She had an antique desk and chair. The bathrooms off each of the bedrooms were just like mine.

"Donna, it's beautiful!"

"I know," she said as she gazed over her handiwork.

I noticed a picture on her dresser that I hadn't seen before of a woman in her early thirties. She was an older version of Donna.

"Who is that a picture of?" The question seemed to put a look of sadness on her face, and I wished I hadn't pried.

"It's my mother. Dad gave it to me before I left home. He said he wanted me to have it." That was all she said about it and then went back to directing the tour. "Over here is the other bedroom. It's laid out pretty much the same as this one, but I decorated it differently. What do you think?"

This room had a four-poster bed made of knotty pine and one of those stand-up mirrors on a frame to match. There was also a dressing table and chest of drawers all in knotty pine. On one of the nightstands was a pitcher and bowl set with a dainty little guest towel hanging over the bowl. On the other was a lamp with a shade to match the curtains, which were a winter-white crochet over a sheer of the same color. On the bed was a double wedding ring quilt with pale pink, beige, touches of baby blue, and splashes of pale yellow. It was the prettiest quilt I'd ever seen.

"I hope whoever we find to share the house with will like it."

Now was the time to bring up Patsey. "Let's go down to the kitchen and have a drink I want to tell you about my trip."

While Donna was getting glasses and ice, I told her about stopping at the diner and meeting Patsey. "She and I got to talking, and I asked her where she was going to be staying. She told me she hadn't found anything in her price range, so I told her to call when she gets here, and we'd all get together and discuss her renting our other room. She's our age, and I met her parents, who own the diner. I know I should have waited and talked to you first, but you know me and my big mouth."

"Hey, we need another person, and if you like her, I'm sure I will. I trust your instincts. Is she coming up soon? School starts next week."

"Yes. As a matter of fact, she's riding up with her cousin tomorrow. He has a place here in town, and she was going to stay with him until she found a place. I guess he only has a studio apartment, so he didn't have room for her permanently. He's helping a professor while waiting for a grant to be approved. "

Donna looked questioningly at Dawn. "Why does your voice suddenly change when you talk about him?"

I could feel my cheeks getting red. Donna was not going to leave it alone until I had spilled my guts. I tried to tell Donna about Jimmy, the tall, dark, and handsome cousin of Patsey Connors. We talked and laughed while eating junk food until midnight.

"Well, what do you think?" Donna asked.

The smile on my face let her know how pleased I was." I gotta tell ya, this day has worn me out. I have got to get some sleep before I drop off right here." Dawn said while yawning.

"Me too I'm so glad you finally got here."

I had only brought in the bare necessities from my car, but tomorrow was another day and the rest could wait until then. I felt completely at home in my new room, but I had a hard time finally falling asleep. I kept seeing Jimmy's face and his captivating smile, not to mention the body of a man who had obviously taken good care of it. What had gotten a hold of me? I had never reacted this way to anyone before, and he probably couldn't care less about me. I finally drifted off, but when I woke up, I felt a little embarrassed at the steamy dreams I had had. I hadn't been able to get Jimmy off my mind. It was so new to have this immediate reaction to a man like this, I didn't quite know how to handle it.

The meeting with Donna and Patsey went pretty much as I had expected, and it was decided that she would move in. Getting to know the area and starting school took up most of my time, but there were moments when thoughts of a tall, dark, handsome man still lingered in the back of my mind.

CHAPTER FOUR

I missed home, Mom, Dad, and Whitney so much. I was long overdue to reach out and get in touch with them, but I decided to write instead. Whitney always loved getting mail.

Dear Whitney,

I didn't know time could go by so fast. It seems like only yesterday that I first pulled into the drive and moved in. I can't believe I've been in school now for six weeks.

After I left home, I stopped at a diner and my waitress was going to be attending college here too. She was so bubbly, and we talked for a while. She needed to find a place to stay, so I told her when she got to town to call and come meet Donna and see if she could be our third roommate. This part is just a bonus, she was riding here with her tall, dark, and handsome cousin, Jimmy. He works at the college with a professor. His field is in agriculture. I almost changed my classes so I could sit and stare at him, but I decided it was probably not a good idea.

Patsey and Donna get along great; I cannot wait until you meet her. She's a great roommate. She's clean and neat, and she loves this house. She said she had never lived in such a big place before. She has almost got the yard in shape too. You won't believe it, but she has even gotten Donna and me working in the rose garden. I think that girl could do anything she set her mind to.

Jimmy helped Patsey move in, but as luck would have it, neither Donna nor I were home. We both had classes, and since then, things have been so hectic. I thought maybe I'd run into him on campus, but so far not a sign of him. I found out more about him from Patsey. She says he wants to get a grant to go to some third-world country and teach them new ways to farm so that they can have a better life. Somehow that even makes him more interesting. Donna met a nice guy already— Frank Kellums. She met him in her computer class. It's so ironic; he's going for a law degree. Since her dad is a lawyer too, maybe that will help her dad accept him. He's taking his prelaw courses, and by the time he has his two years in, they will have added an extension of the state university right here in Monroe so he can finish up there. Donna is so excited that she can get her teaching degree here without having to move. What's going on with school? When Mary brought my things here, she told Donna you're graduating early; I think she said in two more months. Is there gonna be a party? Let me know so I can make plans to be there. I miss you all. How's Dad doing? Is he still trying to get you to ride Queenie? Give her a lump of sugar for me. Write soon! I've gotta hit the books now.

Love ya,
Dawn

Just as I was finishing my letter, I heard the front door open, and someone come up the stairs. When I got to my door, there stood Donna with the biggest smile I've ever seen. She was almost bursting with excitement.

"What on earth is it?"

"I know you're gonna think I'm crazy. I mean, we haven't known each other long but,"

she paused and just beamed with joy.

"Would you hurry up and tell me before you bust a gut?"

"Frank asked me to marry him, and I said yes. Dawn, I have no doubts; he's everything I've always wanted in a husband. He's smart, and kind, and affectionate, and guess what? He loves me, and I love him. Well, speak. But please be happy for me. "

"I am so happy, but you haven't known him very long. I mean, how do you know for sure he's the one?"

"I know this seems crazy, but I just know that this is the man I want to spend the rest of my life with. I don't know how to explain it. I have absolutely no doubts."

"I can see in your face how he must make you feel."

As we were jumping up and down, Patsey came running up the stairs out of breath.

"Is something wrong? The front door was wide open and—" Before she could finish, she could tell that whatever was going on, it was good news.

We all went downstairs to the kitchen— that's where you talk about anything as important as this. Donna tried to tell us all over again how wonderful Frank was and how happy she was. I have to admit, I was more than a little envious of her, but she deserved to be happy, and my day would come.

"Hey, let's have a cookout and invite some friends over to celebrate," Patsey suggested.

"That's a great idea, Patsey. We haven't had anyone over since we moved in."

"Okay, who will we ask?" Dawn wondered.

Knowing already it would please Dawn, Patsey said if it's okay, I'd like to ask Jimmy to come. I haven't seen him since he moved me in here."

The smile on my face let her know it was more than okay.

"We could ask Sharon and Gene, Diane and Tommy, Linda, and how about Connor? He's such a nice guy. That's probably enough for our first party."

"Sharon and Gene are in most of our classes, and they are such a cute couple. Linda works with me at the restaurant, said Patsey, "we get along great. Connor from the bookstore is so sweet."

We planned our menu and decided to have the party as soon as possible. We had to pick a Saturday that Patsey didn't work. She had taken a part-time job at a little restaurant just two blocks from the house called the Maple Street Café. It was a hangout for college kids.

I thought we should toast this happy occasion, so we did with milk and cheesecake, which was about all there was in the refrigerator. There was no way I could concentrate on books tonight.

"Oh, damn, I have a test in the morning," Donna said. "I have no choice. You two can stay down here and talk about me, but we engaged women must be responsible." At that, both Patsey and I threw our paper plates at her. Donna went up the stairs singing, "I feel pretty, oh so pretty."

"If you don't cut that out, we'll make sure there's cake on those plates next time."

Patsey started cleaning up our mess, and I pitched in to help. I told Patsey that I couldn't wait to tell Whitney the news, but I didn't think this was letter worthy. I believe this called for a phone call.

Patsey said, "I can't wait to meet your sister. I feel like I already know her from seeing her pictures and, you do talk about her a lot."

———#———

CHAPTER FIVE

A couple of weeks later, Donna and I were talking about Frank, of course.

"When do you think you'll have your wedding?"

"If it were just up to me, it would be tomorrow, but Frank is sensible. We decided the best time would be in two years—in June, of course. That way he'll be halfway through school, and he will just have to prepare for his bar exams. Frank had to postpone college during the last semester of last year, to go home to help his mom she had fallen and broken her hip. His dad's law firm kept him busy, and Frank insisted. She was appreciative that he came. He took her to therapy, cooked, and basically everything she had always done. She's now able to take care of things, and he got to start again this year. It's just the three of them, and they're a very close family. You'll never believe where they live? They live in Pekin. Can you believe he grew up fifteen miles from me? ""As a matter of fact, I'll bet Daddy knew his dad. My Frank has heard of Daddy and can't wait to meet him. He even wanted to go to him and ask for his approval on the marriage, but I explained it would be too much of a shock and that I'd better be the one to tell him. Daddy called me last week and said he had to travel through here tomorrow. He is going to take me to lunch, so I guess I'll do it then. Think good thoughts for me. I'll be a nervous wreck 'til it's done."

"Everything will be fine. All your dad wants is for you to be happy." said Dawn even though she didn't believe it herself.

"I know, but he doesn't have a great outlook on the whole marriage thing."

I knew Donna was referring to her parents' marriage, but I had learned to tread softly when it came to mentioning her mother.

Donna said, "Well I'd love to sit and talk, but I can't, damn it. See ya before I leave."

I puttered around for a while trying to decide whether to call Whitney now or wait until I could tell her the news. Oh, what the hell, I could call her twice. After I dialed the phone, I got her voicemail, so I left a message and vowed to myself to try and call that night. Then my mind wandered. I'm gonna call Mom Dawn muttered. I thought about my dad and what he was doing. He would probably already be out and about. Just then, Mom answered.

"Hi, Mom, it's Dawn."

"Oh, I haven't forgotten your voice yet. Is anything wrong?" Ida said.

"Mom, you'll never change. You always think phone calls are bad news. No, there's nothing wrong. I just missed you all, and I wanted to catch Whitney before she left the house."

"I'm sorry, but you missed her. She's always busy, either with Mary or school. Have you texted her?" Dawn sighed, "yes, it goes unanswered. I thought maybe I'd have better luck on the home phone. "

——//——

CHAPTER SIX

I started thinking about the differences in the way Whitney and I had been brought up, as opposed to the way Donna had been raised, she had been brought up by her dad and various housekeepers. She didn't have her mom like we did.

She longed for a mother's love, so she shared our mother. Donna would confide in mom. Mom would tell Donna, she felt like she had three daughters, and that pleased Donna.

Her dad wasn't really the neighborly type, so not many people in town really knew him. He traveled a lot for business. If material things counted, he spoiled Donna. She never really wanted all the things he bought her. Donna actually seemed embarrassed having so much. She would often give things to friends less fortunate. She never acted snobbish or different than anyone else.

I could tell she was nervous about telling her dad about being engaged.

She knew her dad hated her mother but never felt comfortable enough to discuss it with him. Donna would talk to me about it sometimes, but she thought there was a lot more to it than the little her dad had told her. With everyone else Donna was right up front with people. She wasn't rude or hurtful, but if you asked her a question, she would give you her honest opinion.

She longed to have a complete family and to be a mom. I only prayed she wasn't rushing into being married so that would come to pass.

A couple of days had gone by, and I still had no answers to my texts, so I decided I'd call Whitney after my classes.

———//———

I walked out to sit out in the gazebo. It was a nice day, and I'd been indoors all day at school.

I dialed our home number, because I was getting worried, and of course Mom answered.

"Hi, honey. Two calls in one week—you must be homesick."

I laughed and said, "Of course I miss home, but I called because Whitney has not been answering my texts." Is she okay?"

"She's not sick if that's what you mean, but she is so busy, she hardly sleeps. Let me take her the phone."

As Whitney got on the phone, I could hardly hear her. She didn't sound like herself; she seemed out of breath.

"Hi, sis. How's everything going?"

"Pretty good, just a little hectic." she sighed. "I want to know what's up with you and early graduation. I know we talked about the possibility, but that was back when I first got here, and you haven't mentioned it since then." Dawn asked.

"Yeah, they started looking over my credits and the extra credits that I had picked up during the summers and called me in and gave me the choice. I wasn't going to bother, but then I mentioned it to Mary. She told me if I did graduate early, she had an opportunity for me that I shouldn't pass up. So, we talked, and I tell you, I'm still reeling from her proposition."

There was silence for a while, and then I heard something. Dawn said, "what was that noise? Are you gonna tell me what the proposition is?"

"I was just opening the refrigerator and grabbing some juice.

Okay, if you're not sitting, you had better sit now. Mary has been approached to do a series of articles and possibly a book in London, England, and she needs an assistant. She wants me, can you believe it? We'll be gone approximately three years, maybe longer. She has arranged for me to be able to take some journalism courses at the university there." Whitney continued, "she said the experience will give my career a big boost. Some of the names of people she mentioned we'll be working with, I've only dreamed of meeting, let alone working with. Dawn, are you still there?"

I could hardly speak. Of course, the thought of not seeing Whitney for an extended length of time bothered me, but I was mostly just overwhelmed.

"Dawn?"

"I'm here. I can't believe it, and I'm in shock. Why didn't you call me and tell me all of this? I have been texting you almost daily with no answers. I was worried."

Whitney replied, "I'm sorry, I should have called, I just needed to process it all.

It's funny, I was gonna call you today. Mom, Daddy, Mary, and I just made the final decision last night. There is no way I can pass on this, I'm just a bit overwhelmed. "

"Of course you can't let this pass you by. You might never get an opportunity like this again. It's just—I'm gonna miss you so much." Dawn said.

Whitney answered, "Me too, but you are going to be there for the next two years, and who knows? Maybe you can fly to London. Wouldn't that be great?"

"Right, like I can afford that." said Dawn.

"Well, maybe by then I can—ha!" Whitney laughed.

"When do you have to leave? Am I gonna see you before you go?" Dawn asked sadly.

"Actually, I was planning on coming up to see you and Donna in two weeks because I have to leave the next weekend. I could sure use those extra clothes that you took with you." Whitney said slyly.

"Oh, I'm so sorry I had to have clothes to wear. I'm not going to a nudist college, you know." Dawn replied sarcastically.

We laughed and talked some more about this and that, and I forgot to even talk to Mom again. She won't be pleased with me, but she won't call back because she is a miser about long-distance calls, and she still refuses to use a cell phone. Oh well. I'll talk to her in the next few days when I call back to tell Whitney about Donna's news. I'm not sure it will have as much impact now with her exciting news, but she will be surprised. Maybe then Daddy would be home, and I could talk to everyone. I couldn't stand it any longer, so I ran upstairs to tell Donna about Whitney. She was in the shower, so I went out to the gazebo and sat thinking about Whitney and how much fun we'd had as children.

CHAPTER SEVEN

Whitney was always the curious and adventurous one. I can hardly remember her without a pad of paper and a pencil tucked in her pocket. She used to interview everyone. I remember how embarrassed Mom and Dad were the time she walked up to Pastor Michaels after church service, one Sunday and asked, pad in hand, "Pastor Michaels, how did you get started in this business?" Mom just smiled as she took Whitney by the hand to the car.

"Sweetheart, you can't just walk up and pry into people's business."

"Why not?"

"Just because I say so!"

Whitney knew that was the end of that conversation. When Mom said, just because I say so, then that was that.

Back then it had only piqued her curiosity, she was going to find out what secrets he was hiding, and it had only made her more determined to get his story. Living in a small town, people label you right from the start. Pretty soon, when they'd see Whitney coming with her pad and pencil, they'd say, Here comes the press, and laugh. It didn't bother her, though. She'd just say, I have a job to do, and there are stories to be told. At eight years old, I don't know who she thought she worked for. Most everyone took it in stride and answered her questions and then excused themselves by always needing to be someplace in hurry.

As kids, you couldn't help but hear the town gossip about one person or another. This always aroused Whitney's curiosity, so one day she decided to pay a visit to the local "loose woman," as Mom called her, Betty Jo Simpson, let me just put it this way: Mom confiscated her notes on Ms. Simpson and gave Whitney so many chores to do she didn't have time to do any interviews for a good long while. It was funny, though. Every time we'd run across Betty Jo Simpson, on the street or in the grocery store, she'd just smile and wink at Whitney. At the same time, some of the married men in town turned red and acted a little nervous around us.

I guess the closest I ever was to my sister was when I was eleven. I got really sick with a high fever for no clear reason.Old Doc Armstrong even admitted me to the hospital over in Pembrooke. I'm not sure how long I was there, but it must have been serious. They ran all kinds of tests and couldn't come up with any reason for me being so sick. Grandma Pracket finally convinced Mom and Dad that I'd be better off at home in my own bed with family taking care of me.

Grandma Pracket always had her home remedies from way back, and she started tending to me herself. Once I was home, they said Whitney would sit in my room talking to me and reading stories to me until Mom came and chased her out. When I finally came around, there she was chatting away. Just as quickly as I had gotten sick, I started getting better. Old Doc Armstrong came by to check on me, and he told Mom and Dad, "If there's anything I've learned in all these years of

doctoring', it's just there aren't any hard and fast answers to healing."
Granny said her herbal potions, prayer, and the loving care of family
was all I needed.

I was still a little weak, and Mom and Dad decided the family needed some time to relax. We all went to my Uncle Bill's cabin on Lake
Potomac for a week.

I knew Whitney would have rather been running through the
woods or fishing, but instead she sat at the edge of the lake with me.
She even got Mom's okay to take me out in the little rowboat Uncle Bill
left at the cabin.

She sounded so grown-up when she said, "You just sit back and
relax. I'll do all the rowing."

The morning of our last day at the lake, I woke up feeling like my
old self. Whitney and I explored the woods and picked a whole buck-
et full of berries. That night, we had a weenie roast, and Daddy made
homemade ice cream that we topped with our fresh berries. It was great.
It was then that Whitney gave me a poem that my grandma had written
when she was twenty.

Purpose
Since I was a kid, I knew for me
The Lord had a purpose that I would see
I knew not whether it be great or small
Only that when I knew, I'd share it with all
My learning and faith at times have faltered
But I knew my life would definitely be altered
If we can be patient and believe in the Lord above
Whatever we ask, he'll grant out of love
Ora Pracket

Whitney said, "maybe that's where I got my love of writing from."

CHAPTER EIGHT

I started to remember the last time I had run into Jimmy. He had been on campus talking rather intimately with a tall blonde. He caught me staring at them, so of course he walked over. Embarrassed doesn't even cover it. He turned to the blonde and introduced me as the young woman his cousin roomed with. Like I was a kid or something. I was so mad; I didn't trust myself to speak. Who did he think he was, anyway? It had been weeks ago, but it still made me just as mad.

I suddenly heard someone coming around the house and figured it was Donna. To my unmistakable shock, it was Jimmy. It was as if I had conjured him up out of thin air.

"Hi there. I hope I didn't scare you. I knocked at the front door, but no one answered so I thought I'd check around here."

"I must say you did startle me. I thought it was Donna coming to tell me she was leaving for school. Are you looking for Patsey?"

"As a matter of fact, I was gonna use that as an excuse, but I was hoping to see you."

"Well, you're in luck. Here I am." Right then, I realized I had put on my gown and robe after classes. "You'll have to excuse my appearance. I don't always hang out in my pajamas, but it has been quite an eventful day."

"You look just fine to me."

"Oh really? What about Muffy, or Buffy, or whatever your girlfriend's name is?"

"I'm not sure I know what you mean, and why do you sound so grumpy?"

"Oh, you man, you!"

Just then Donna came around the corner as I was running toward the back door.

"Hi, Jimmy. Dawn, what's wrong? What did you do to her?"

Jimmy just shook his head and turned to leave. "Women, you're all alike!"

I firmly decided to put that arrogant jerk out of my mind. Every time I noticed him around campus, I would duck behind a building or a tree or whatever to avoid him.

I was acting like a middle schooler. I would keep avoiding him, nor give a shit about what he thought of me. Muffy, Buffy, or whoever she was could have him, and it was time I grew a pair and got on with my life!

CHAPTER NINE

I joined study groups and threw myself into my schoolwork. We had postponed the cookout so Whitney could come, but as it turned out, the only face-to-face we got with Whitney was FaceTime. Mary had to get to London with her sooner than expected. I was sad, but Whitney was so excited that I sucked it up and rode her high. For one reason or another, we kept having to postpone the cookout, which was fine with me. I didn't have to endure being around Jimmy.

Finally, there was half a day of school, so I went home, changed into comfy clothes, and sat in our gazebo looking at our now beautiful yard. I was lost in daydreams when I heard someone out front. Patsey was working, and Donna was with Frank. I headed to the front of the house, and standing at our front door was Jimmy.

"Are you looking for Patsey?"

He turned and smiled at me, and my cheeks started feeling really warm.

"I just got to thinking that I have not been keeping a good eye on you girls, so…No, that's not true. I wanted to clear the air with you."

"Whatever do you mean?"

"I think you may have gotten the wrong impression of me, and it was probably my fault."

Trying to act unfazed, I said, "I don't know what you're talking about."

All he said was, "Muffy or Buffy?"

"I'm sorry. I don't know your girlfriend's name."

"She's not my girlfriend. She's one of my friend's girlfriend." Jimmy said. This threw Dawn, she began thinking about how childish she had been. She was still mad about how he introduced her. She just stood there with this stunned look on her face.

She realized he was still standing there and asked, "what do you want?"

I wondered if I could take you to dinner tonight? That is, if you're not already booked."

"No, I'm not, and I think I'd like that."

"Great. I'll come by around eight, then."

"I'll be here."

The rest of the day was a waste for me. All I could think about was tonight and what I was going to wear. I decided I'd take a walk and stop by Maple St. Café to see Patsey. I wanted to ask Patsey if she had talked to Jimmy about the party. I also wanted to tell her about our date.

All Patsey said was, "Well, it's about time. I swear that boy is as slow as pond water. You can ask him to the party tonight."

We didn't really have a set date for the cookout yet. When he picked me up, he suggested it was a great night for a walk by the lake. The night was beautiful, and the moon was shining down on the water.

We sat down on the bench, and he took my hand and slowly started to speak.

"I don't want you to think I'm some sort of jerk, but from the first time I saw you, you're all I've been able to think about. You are something. I can't believe my uncle asked me to watch out for you and Patsey. I keep wondering who's gonna protect you from me."

"Jimmy, I'm not a kid. I have feelings too. I've got to admit, I've done my fair share of thinking about you too. I don't think I want to be protected from you."

He took me in his arms and just held on to me so gently, brushing my hair from my face. We just sat in each other's arms, content to be together for now.

Jimmy said, "I bet you're getting hungry for that dinner I promised you."

I just shrugged.

"I've got a surprise for you. Patsey's dad, my uncle, has a cabin just up there that I want you to see. I promise I have only good intentions." We went into the cabin, and to my surprise, he had dinner ready for us.

"Wow, you cook?"

"It's nothing fancy, just country cookin'. I learned from my mom."

———//———

When I got home, the whole house was lit up. Donna and Patsey had the stereo on, singing and shuffling through the CDs. They gave me a little sideways glance and smile and tried to sing, "It's raining men, hallelujah raining men." I turned their music down a touch, and they told me they were picking out the music for our party.

"Where's Jimmy? Did you wear him out? You sassy wench, you."

I swatted Donna with a pillow. "He had to get home. He has an early class tomorrow."

"Well!"

"Well, what?"

"Give, girl. You have been waiting around for weeks-thinking of ways to torture him and that's all we have heard, what a jerk Jimmy is and mumbling about somebody named Buffy."

"You are just plain wicked, Donna MacIntosh, and I'm not sure you're any better, Miss Patsey Connors."

"Okay then, we'll be forced to make up our version of what happened."

I just shook my head and told them it was everything I had hoped it would be. "He was a gentleman."

"Okay, if we aren't getting any dirt, let's get on with the plans. We only have a few days!"

"So, you set a date for the cookout?" I didn't invite Jimmy

Yet because I didn't know when it would finally happen. "We decided no time's gonna be perfect, so we're just going for it. It's in four days, and Patsey and I have called everybody on our list. All we have to do is shop for groceries and prepare the side dishes to go with the burgers and chicken."

CHAPTER 10

The lunch meeting with Donna's dad was today. I hope all goes well, but with Mr. MacIntosh you never knew what to expect.

If I knew Donna and I did, once she's made her mind up, she'll get what she wants.

The next day after class when I got home, I could hear Donna in the kitchen singing.

"Donna, can I assume that everything went well with your father today?"

"It was touch and go when I first told him. He brought up what you would expect. He was a little angry as he said, 'You don't really know him. It's only been a few months, and you're too young to get married.' Then his mood changed to guilt-tripping. He said he'd brought me up alone, and he wasn't sure marriage worked for anyone. He finally looked at me. I had tears running down my cheeks, and he was at once quiet. He finally gave us his blessing with a bit of doubt behind his words. I just decided that was good enough for me."

"I know you're relieved to have that behind you."

"I really am. Now I can announce it to the world." Then Donna went to the front door and yelled for all to hear, *"I'm getting married to Frank Kellums!"*

A boy going by on his bike nearly fell off, and we had to drag her back in before she scared the whole neighborhood. Both of us were laughing so hard I almost peed my pants.

The next four days flew by, and everyone had RSVP'd for the party. The food was prepared, and the house was spotless, thanks to Patsey. The yard was not perfect, but it looked pretty good.

Readying the food and house was a snap compared to deciding what to wear. We had all changed at least four times, and as the doorbell rang and the first guest arrived, I still wasn't sure I had chosen the right outfit. Each group that arrived wanted a tour of the house. The favorite thing was the old player piano.

It seemed we made the right choice in our guest list. Everyone was getting along and having fun. We all gathered around the piano and sang along to the old rolls of music that had come with the piano.

I was wondering where Jimmy was. Everyone else was there.

Jimmy finally came through the door, and we all went to welcome him and get him a drink. I decided to take him on a tour of the house myself. We toured the upstairs since that's the only part he hadn't seen before, except for Patsey's room I didn't notice how perfect her room was when I was unloading all her stuff. This is the best house she's ever lived in," Jimmy said. Then we went into Donna's room. He stopped and picked up a picture that was sitting on Donna's nightstand. He looked at me as if he had seen a ghost. He turned to me with confusion and anger.

"Where did she get this?"

"It's a picture of her mother. She left when Donna was almost three."

He put it back and then left the room and the house without a word.

I tried to go after him, but it was no use. His Corvette was screeching out of the driveway. I went out to the front porch and stared out into the night, totally confused and angry that he had run out with no explanation. I tried his cell phone, several times, but it went right to voicemail. I was pissed!

"Fine! Mr. Connors, I don't need some maniac in my life."

Just then Patsey walked out. "Hey, we've been looking for you. Where's Jimmy?"

"He's gone, thank god he's nuts." With that, Dawn stormed back in the house, leaving a confused Patsey following behind her. Dawn stopped so quickly Patsey nearly ran into her.

"I'm sorry, Patsey. I shouldn't have taken my anger out on you. We're having a party. Let's go have some fun."

"Do you want to talk about what ever Jimmy did?"

"No! Absolutely not.

I thought to myself why would he react like that over a picture of Donna's mother? I wonder if he doesn't like Donna for yelling at him that day I stormed off, but what does the picture have to do with anything?

CHAPTER 11

The weeks that followed proved that trying to figure out the night of the party was giving me a headache. He had not answered any texts or calls.

Jimmy finally managed to find me while I was sitting out in the courtyard at school. I wasn't paying any attention to my surroundings, and he sat down beside me. When he said my name, I couldn't move.

He said, "I'm sorry I left the party so quickly without an explanation."

"I'm just asking you to trust in me, and soon I will explain everything to you. I'm going to visit my mom tomorrow, and I'd like you to go with me. I want to leave early in the morning, so would you consider staying at my uncle's cabin by the lake tonight?"

I was stunned, but I managed to say, "Yes, I would like that."

I quickly packed an overnight bag and left a note for the girls saying I would be away for the next few days.

Jimmy arrived to pick me up and put my bag in the car. He seemed anxious.

My head started reeling. This would be a first for me. Before I could say anything, Jimmy said, "There are two bedrooms, if you are nervous about that." He seemed to be less anxious as we drove.

I decided I'd better say something. I told him we'd talk it all out when we got to the cabin.

We arrived at the cabin, and almost before we got inside, he grabbed me and hugged me so tightly. It was as though he needed me to be with him, even if just to hold me close and not be alone.

There was a chill in the air, so he built a fire in the fireplace. We sat around it while we ate the sandwiches and chips, he had brought with him.

He seemed in deep thought, so I didn't say anything. He seemed to snap out of it and turned to smile at me. He came closer and kissed me. My whole insides were on fire. I had never felt like this before. I didn't want the kiss to end. He pulled away, cupped my face in his hands, and said, "I need you, but I will follow your lead."

I pulled him closer and kissed him until all I felt was passion and need.

We didn't need that second bedroom!

When I woke up, Jimmy wasn't there beside me, but I could hear him in the kitchen. He came in with a cup of coffee and a giant smile on his face. He leaned over to kiss me.

"If I stay here any longer, we'll never get to my mom's." He lingered a little longer and then stood up. She could see the evidence of lust, so he turned toward the kitchen "There's some bacon and eggs in the kitchen."

I looked around for something to put on. He saw my dilemma and tossed me his robe.

The night had been like a dream. It felt right and comfortable and amazing.

We finished our breakfast, the first one a man had made for me. He said, "I put some fresh towels for you in the bathroom. I've got a few things to put in the car, so take your time and then we'll be on our way."

I liked the way his robe felt against my skin. It had his masculine scent on it. I got my clothes and toiletries out of my bag and headed to the shower. I heard his phone ring and hesitated for a few moments wondering if I should go pick it up, but then I heard Jimmy talking on his cell in the kitchen. It must have been his mom because he said, "Yes, I'm still coming. I'll be leaving in a little while. I'm bringing someone with me, and you're gonna love her. She's pretty terrific. I'll tell you all about it when we get there."

The way he described me to his mom made me smile. While I was standing in the shower, letting the water run in my face, I began to think about last night and felt myself getting aroused. I thought maybe I'd better turn the water on cold. I needed to get a move on so we could be on our way. I finally appeared from the bathroom, dressed and ready to go. Jimmy had made the bed and was sitting having another cup of coffee in the kitchen.

"Hey, beautiful. Ready to go?" He gave me a kiss and looked at me with that smile that I had come to treasure.

"I'm all set. Let's hit the road."

The drive was through the most beautiful country I'd ever seen. I wanted to talk to Jimmy about his reaction to the picture of Donna's mother, but I didn't want him to get spooked again. It just all seemed so strange. Here was a woman that Donna hadn't seen for fifteen or sixteen years, and now someone thought they recognized her—now I was getting spooked.

CHAPTER 12

Patsey was in shock when Dawn told her about Jimmy recognizing the woman in the picture, she really had never noticed it, but she was rarely in Donna's room. She was certainly going to look at it when Frank and Donna went out. When Patsey was finally alone and saw the picture, she nearly fell to the floor. "Aunt Jessie, much younger but definitely, Aunt Jessie." Holy shit Patsey wailed. "How on earth am I supposed to act like I don't know who she is?"

CHAPTER 13

"You're awfully quiet. Is something wrong?"

"You and Donna have known each other for a long time, haven't you?"

Dawn answered, "We've known each other all our lives. Donna and I have been best friends all through school. She sort of adopted my mother as her own."

"What happened to her mother?"

"Why are you all of a sudden so curious about Donna?" Dawn asked. "Who do you think that picture was?" Dawn asked.

Jimmy replied, "That was my mother, I have a picture just like it."

Dawn couldn't speak. She just stared at Jimmy with wide eyes.

"Maybe that gives you some insight as to why I rushed out of the party."

Dawn answered, in shock, "I just know from hearing my parents talk about it because we were too little to really remember ourselves. Let's see, Donna was about three years old,

and her mom left town and never came back.

I know Donna has always wanted to find her mother and at least see her and be able to talk to her. It's funny—, she's never really felt bitter toward her mom. Her dad is a successful lawyer with his own firm in Bradleyville , he traveled a lot and was a wealthy man. He tried to over compensate for Donna's mother leaving and the fact that he spent so much time working. He gave Donna everything, but oddly enough she's really not your typical spoiled brat. She's very giving and generous. She loves children. I was surprised a little that she came to college. Her real ambition is to get married and have a house full of kids and be a wife and mommy. She and I are a lot alike."

I hadn't realized that I had been going on and on about Donna, and while I was, Jimmy had that strange look on his face again. Well, I didn"t want to spook him, and that was just what I'd done.

"Jimmy, what's wrong? You look just like you did the night at the party."

"Remember how I told you that my mom traveled a lot when I was small?" Jimmy asked.

"Yes, I remember," said Dawn.

"Well, she used to work for a big-shot lawyer who had cases all over, and she would have to travel with him. I remember the last time she was away, she was gone for months and then came home only to leave again in about a week for even longer. I felt sorry for myself and for my dad, but he never got mad or acted sad. He just kept reassuring me that Mommy would be home soon and that she loved us very much. I guess I believed him, or at least I tried to. Finally, when my dad got sick, mom quit her job to take care of us and never left again. It is something I've not let myself think about for a long time but seeing that picture the night of the party was unbelievable. You see, my dad had that very same picture. He kept it on his dresser until the day he died." reported Jimmy.

I just sat there with my mouth open and a blank look on my face. Then, as if compelled to speak, I blurted out, "I can't believe it. I just can't believe it. Your mother is Donna's mother! Then you and Donna are half brother and sister. This is—" I didn't finish the sentence because I couldn't begin to describe what this was. "How does this make you feel?" she asked

"I'm not sure exactly. I know I love my mother, no matter what her past. No one could have given my father better care for all those years—or me, for that matter. She is one of the most giving people I've ever known. Anyone in our little town that needs a helping hand, she is right there to cook or clean or tend to kids. It's like she almost has too much love to give. I know I'll have to talk to her about this because she can read me like a book, and she'll know I'm trying to keep something from her. I don't want her to worry, and I don't want to hurt her, but if Donna is her daughter—and I'm sure she is—I know she would want to see her, especially if Donna wants to see her, I don't know my mother's reasons for why she left her daughter and stayed with us, but I know my mother and she had to have had no other choice."

"This was probably not the best time to bring a stranger home, Jimmy." Dawn said.

"Dawn, I am so sorry to drag you into this, but I really need you with me. All you have to do is be yourself and keep an open mind."

"I'll do my best. I don't want your mother to feel trapped." replied Dawn.

"I don't either." said Jimmy.

The rest of the ride was fairly quiet and went by much too fast.

CHAPTER 14

"We're here. Just relax. You look like you're about to go to the gas chamber."

There waiting on the porch stood the mother of not only her best friend but the mother of her boyfriend.

"Jimmy boy, you're a sight for sore eyes. I have missed you so much." She hugged Jimmy as if he'd been gone for ages. "And who is this precious girl you have with you?"

"Mom, this is Dawn Pracket. She and Patsey are roommates."

"Oh, I wish Patsey had come. I haven't seen her in such a long time. Dawn, darlin', come on in. I have lunch all prepared. You two must be starving."

"Mom, you always think everyone is starving."

"Oh, Jimmy, quit teasing me."

The house was a modest farmhouse, but it was so clean it sparkled. Downstairs, there was a big kitchen, and a large living room with a wood-burning stove in it, a small bathroom, and a little bedroom just off the living room. Upstairs, there were three more small bedrooms and a bathroom.

There was a big front porch with a rocker and a swing. Off of the kitchen, there was what my grandmother used to call a summer kitchen where she did her laundry and canning. It had a big chest freezer that I was sure was full of frozen homegrown vegetables and frozen meat.

You could smell the food she'd been cooking all through the house. She'd probably made all of Jimmy's favorites. There was a big chocolate cake sitting on the kitchen counter. I think I gained ten pounds just smelling it all.

"Mom, you are somethin'. Chicken and dumplings, fresh pole beans, and are these tomatoes out of the garden? Let's eat the chocolate cake first!"

She acted like she was going to slap Jimmy's hand. "You never change. You may have grown up, but you still want your dessert first. You sit down here and eat a proper meal then you can have cake."

"Okay, but one day you might give in and let me have my cake first, so I can't quit trying

Strangely enough, I felt completely at ease watching how sweet Jimmy and his mother were together. For a while, I forgot that this was also Donna's missing mother.

"Jimmy, will you ask the blessing?"

Jimmy asked the blessing, and as he finished, he said, "We love you, Dad."

I thought I'd cry, but Jimmy didn't seem sad. As a matter of fact, he seemed happy. And his mother was beaming. After all, she had her son home, and it was an affirmation of family love that the three of them had shared.

"The sooner we eat, the sooner we get cake," Jimmy added.

"You are bad, Jimmy."

We all ate and talked about school and about Patsey. Jimmy and his mom talked about what he had to do to repair the roof. As I sat and ate and listened, I realized I didn't even know this lady's name. She was just Jimmy's mom. Then all kinds of questions started popping into my head, like was she married to both Donna's father and Jimmy's dad at the same time? How could this sweet lady have left a small child and never try to see her again? Donna—how was I going to handle this with her? I knew it wasn't my place to tell her, but somebody had to. After all, she was my oldest and dearest friend, and I didn't want her hurt., so Whoever broke this news to her had better do it right. Then I got pulled back into the. conversation.

"You got awfully quiet."

"Oh, I'm just enjoying this good food."

"I'll show you around the place while Jimmy does his repairs, if you'd like."

"That would be great. You know, I don't even know your first name. Jimmy just introduced you as Mom."

"My name is Jessie."

"Good, now I won't have to say 'Hey, you,' no thanks to you, sir." Dawn said to Jimmy.

"Don't you two go picking on me, or I won't share my cake."

"I believe I'll have to wait awhile for mine anyway. I'm stuffed. It's been a long time since I've had good home cookin'. I'm afraid I made a pig of myself." "I like to see people enjoy their food. A lot of young people these days are on a diet, trying to fit into a size 0. I think that's hogwash." Donna snickered at Jessie's comments. She sounded a lot like mom.

Jessie took her to a lovely bedroom where she had had Jimmy put her things. The view from the window was breathtaking. There were fields and trees with wild flowers here and there. It was truly peaceful.

Jessie and I started to clear the table.

"Where are you from, Dawn?"

I got a lump in my throat and half stuttered, "Bradleyville."

Jessie didn't say anything for a while. The silence was nerve-racking. I tried to make idle chitchat about how much I loved the house and this and that. I even told her how I had met Patsey and how she came to be my roommate. She smiled and added a remark here and there, and then she asked me how long I'd lived in Bradleyville.

"I've lived there all of my life." Then I opened my mouth and stuck my foot right in. "Have you ever been to Bradleyville?"

Well, it was said, and there was nothing I could do about it.

"Yes, I believe I have. Let's leave the rest of this mess for later. I want to show you my garden and the flowerbed that Jimmy planted for me. They are beautiful, some strange hybrids that he developed."

Then they went outside, and Dawn could hear hammering, Jessie said," I hope that boy doesn't fall off the roof, then I'll feel bad for not letting him have his cake first." They both laughed.

By the time they made it around to the front porch, Jimmy came walking his way out of the barn.

When he got to the porch, he said, with a satisfied look on his face," I believe you owe me my cake, my job is done."

Dawn offered to help Jessie with the cake, but she told them to just sit on the swing and she would get it.

A young boy came out of the barn. "I'm all done, Mrs. McCoy, I fed the animals and cleaned up around the barn."

"Okay, Tommy. Thanks, and I'll see you tomorrow afternoon. Tell your mom I said hello and to get some fresh vegetables when she needs them."

"Okay, I will. Bye

It was great to be riding again. It made me feel so free with the wind blowing in my face and the smell of hay in the fields.

Jimmy had forgotten some tools on the roof and had to get back up there and retrieve them.

Jessie walked over to where Jimmy was working and called to him, "Jimmy."

"Yes, Mom, what do you need?"

"I need for you to come down for a while."

Jimmy climbed down the ladder, and his mom just looked at him and said, "Jimmy, you know how very much I loved your father, don't you?"

"Of course I do, Mom."

"And you know that I love you more than life itself."

"Yes, Mom. What's wrong?"

"How close are you and Dawn?"

"I think I love her, Mom."

"She told me she's from Bradleyville." She looked into Jimmy's eyes, and she could tell he knew or at least knew something. "You know, don't you?"

"Yes, Mom, I think so. I know you have a daughter."

"How did you find out?"

"Donna MacIntosh is Dawn's best friend, and she is living with her and Patsey. I saw that same picture of you that Dad always kept on his dresser on Donna's nightstand."

"Did you say anything to her?"

"No. Dawn and I didn't know what to do."

"Dawn's out riding Duke. You go get her and come in. I need to talk to you both." There were tears in Jessie's eyes as she walked toward the house.

Jimmy ran out and got Lily out of the barn. He didn't even bother to saddle her. He finally caught up with Dawn and told her his mom wanted to talk to them both.

"Are you sure she wants me there? I could just stay outside."

"No, she wants you there. She knows you know as much as I do and that you are Donna's best friend."

They got back and took the horses to the stable. When they went in the house, Jessie was sitting in her rocker looking very sad.

"Come in and sit with me, children. I want to tell you the whole story. It all started some thirty years ago, give, or take a few. I worked in a factory close to here that manufactured, among other things, farm equipment. Your father was the supervisor, and I had worked on the line since I graduated from high school. My family had little money, and only the boys got to go to college. I tried to make up for it by reading everything I could get my hands on. Anyway, it was my birthday, and your daddy and I had been going together for about five years. I was beginning to think he was never going to ask me to marry him. He was a proud man and wanted everything to be exactly right. He said, 'Jessie, by next year I should have enough money to put down on the old Gillespie farm on the hill and we can get married—if you'll have me?' I said, 'Oh, Jim, of course I'll have you, but do we really have to wait? I don't mind working and helping out.' He said, 'You know how I feel about my wife working, and besides, you'll need to be home to care for all those kids of ours.' Jessie blushed and said, "Sam McCoy, you are too old fashioned." ' Then Sam handed me a small, wrapped box with a pink rose bud on top and said, Happy birthday, Jessie, my sweet. It was a small gold ring with a tiny stone but to me it was grander than any I'd ever seen. Sam took the ring out of the box and placed it on my finger. He said, "I'll never love another as long as I live.' And I told him, "Nor I, Sam. I love you so much."

"What that year had in store for us no one could have predicted. Times were hard, and the family who had owned and run the factory since it had started many years ago were forced to sell to a big corporation out of Washington. They wanted to make more military parts and less and less farm equipment. The operation of the factory changed drastically. They came in and automated many of the jobs that had been done by hand, so lots of hardworking, loyal people were let go with no way to make a living. Many of them lost their homes and were devastated. Many of the promises that had been made to them by the earlier owners had been made only verbally with a handshake. Your dad and I kept on, at least at first. He was so angered with the management that he made his feelings known and even formed a group of employees who held meetings to discuss what could be done to fight the system. So many were afraid of fighting management for fear of losing their own jobs and not being able to care for their own families.

"That's when Frank MacIntosh came into the picture. He was the corporation's attorney. He had taken a liking to me from the start and repeatedly asked me out. I made it quite clear that I was engaged and was unavailable, but you could tell he was used to getting what he wanted. Tension in the factory spread throughout the town and beyond. There was talk of a walk out among the employees.

"One evening when I was getting off my shift, Frank MacIntosh followed me to my car. He said, "Jessie, I'd like to talk to you about this trouble at work." Stupidly I agreed to meet him for coffee to discuss it. I thought I could help the situation.

"He picked me up, and we drove to a little restaurant about an hour away, which was fine with me because I didn't want your dad to know. I knew he wouldn't like it. This man was a smooth talker and every bit the convincing attorney. He led me to believe that he cared about the people and that he could help. But when he took me home and I resisted his advances, he looked at me with those cold eyes and said, 'You'll change your mind about me because I've decided I'm going to marry you. "I thought he was insane. The next day at work, I was glad I didn't see him, but what was strange was I hadn't seen Jim either. The whistle blew, and all work stopped. Over the loudspeaker came an announcement: "To all employees, especially the group led by Sam McCoy, we'd like you to know that while you thought he was your friend and had your best interest at heart, it seems he didn't. The police have just taken him away for embezzling company money. Any further grievances should be taken up with our personnel manager. Now let's get back to work and earn our pay.'

"I was absolutely stunned at this absurd accusation. I ran out of that factory and never returned. I found out they had taken Sam to the county jail. They wouldn't let me see him at first, so I just sat and waited. They got tired of me hanging around pestering them, so they finally let me talk to him.

He was devastated. I've never felt so bad for a person in my life. I asked him, "Sam, what happened?' He said, "I don't know. They say they have proof that I stole company money over the years. I don't understand it. How could they have proof of something that never happened? They showed me a bank account in my name from a bank in Sparks. It showed deposits adding up to twenty-five thousand dollars. How can that be? Why are they doing this to me? Is it because I tried to help the people? I'm no threat. Jessie, I didn't do it." I told him, "You do not have to defend yourself to me. I know you did not do anything wrong.' After that day, things got worse and worse. People who had known your dad all their lives turned against him. They started blaming him for all the trouble at the factory, and said he was a trouble maker. It came time for the trial, and the whole town showed up. We hired a local lawyer, but he was no competition for their team of lawyers.

Sam was found guilty and sentenced to prison for no less than ten years. I even sold the ring he had given me to help pay the lawyer, but we didn't stand a chance.

"While in prison, Sam went into a deep depression and even refused to see me or anyone else. His health started to fail. I was worried sick about him. Frank Macintosh still tried to pursue me from time to time, but I repeatedly refused him. I couldn't stand even looking at him.

"I got word that Sam had been put in the prison hospital, and talk was they were afraid he would try to kill himself. I had to do something fast, so I called Frank MacIntosh and asked if he could meet with me. He gloated and said, 'I knew You would come around sooner or later.' I bit my tongue because I knew he was my only hope of helping Jim. He delighted in the fact that I had to come crawling to him for help. He listened to my plea. Then he said, 'Yes, I believe I can help you get McCoy out of prison, but in exchange, you have to marry me.' I told him he was crazy and ran out of his fancy office.

"I went to an attorney and told him of his proposition, but he said we couldn't prove anything. A month later, Sam was still no better— even worse—so I decided I had to give in to him if I was going to save Sam. I called Frank, and he got to work on it right away. The very day that Jim was released from prison, Frank and I were married and left town for a honeymoon. When I refused him in the bedroom, he forced himself on me.

"We didn't return, but instead we lived in Washington. Frank gained increased power and notoriety. I was sure some of his business acquaintances were gangsters. I was out of place in his world of society parties and late dinners. Even with the expensive clothes, I just didn't fit in. I was pleased one day when he came home and told me we were moving to Bradleyville. He said he had a business opportunity in Bradleyville that he couldn't refuse. He had also decided it was time we had a child. Even though I had always wanted children, I couldn't stand the thought of being with him. I also worried about what kind of influence he would have on a child.

"We made the move, and I was happier just to be back in a small town with pleasant people. I had never heard from Sam in all this time, but I heard from a friend that he had bought a little farm—this one. He hadn't married. Sam was a proud man, and he felt like I was better off without him.

"Frank's business was doing well because he had hired a full-time housekeeper. I don't think he trusted that I knew how to entertain his friends properly. I didn't care because it gave me someone to talk to. Her name was Trudy, and she and I became good friends. The next month, Frank had to go away on business, and I had decided to try to see Sam at least to explain what had happened. I missed him so.

"I drove to his house by the directions from my friend. On the way, it started to storm, and I was afraid I wouldn't make it. Some of the roads had been closed due to heavy water. I was determined to see him. When I knocked on his door, I looked like a drowned rat. Sam opened the door, and we just stood there looking at each other. I tried to speak, but nothing came out. Then Sam pulled me in and helped me to dry off. The tears were streaming down my face, and he took me in his arms and held me as if both our lives depended on it. That was the first time I had felt safe and loved in a long time. We talked for hours, and I blurted out the whole story. Then we made love, and that was the night you were conceived. The first thing in the morning, the phone rang, and it was Trudy. She was so upset. She told me that Frank had called. He was coming back early, and he wanted to know where I was. She said, 'Oh, Ms. Jessie, you must come home right away before he gets here.' I told her, 'Okay, Trudy, don't worry. Everything will be fine.' I had hoped I was convincing because I was not at all sure everything would be fine. I was scared to death, and Sam didn't want me to leave. He wanted to protect me and go back and give Frank just what he deserved. I convinced him I would be fine and to let me work things out. I told him to trust me. He said, 'Jessie, now that we've found each other again, I can't bear to lose you.' I told him, 'You won't, my darling. Just be patient for a little while longer.'

"I drove back as fast as I could. I got back just in time for a phone call from Frank. He asked, where were you last night? I called, and there was no answer.' I said, 'Our phone was out of service due to the storm.' He followed up, saying, 'I called this morning, and Trudy said you had already gone out. Where were you so early?' I lied, 'I walked down to get a paper. Ours was all wet, and I just wanted to take a walk.' I hated lies, but somehow when I thought of what he felt about other people's feelings, lying to him did not seem so bad.

"He said, 'I'm stuck about an hour away. The roads are washed out, and I must wait until they're open to get home. Tell Trudy we will be having guests for a few days. Dan Anderson and Belinda, his wife, will be arriving around six tonight. I want a standing rib roast and all the trimmings and have her fix a special dessert too. Dan and I have some business to conduct. You will be there when I get home, won't you?' I said, 'Yes!' He was so sarcastic. During the Andersons stay with us, I learned that Dan Anderson had been involved in the swindle years ago at the factory. Belinda Anderson was quite a drinker, and when she drank, she had a loose tongue.

"I was waiting to tell Frank that I was leaving until after our guests left. Then the morning after they left, I got violently sick to my stomach. I could hardly lift my head off the pillow. I couldn't keep any food down. Trudy insisted on taking me to the doctor.

"I found out I was pregnant. I knew it was Sam's because I hadn't been with Frank in several months. I was thankful for that. He had been too busy setting up his business deals and hadn't forced the issue. I went right home and told Frank I wanted a divorce and was leaving. He was enraged. He told me he'd find me no matter where I went. Then he started shoving me around, and without thinking, I screamed, 'Stop it! You'll hurt the baby. I'm pregnant.' He stopped dead in his tracks and said, 'You are not leaving me with my baby in your belly.' I told him, 'It's not yours!' If Trudy hadn't come in, I think he would have killed me, but she did, and I took advantage of the moment and ran out of the house. I drove straight to Sam's farm. I didn't hear from Frank, nor did he find me that summer. You were born, and we thought we could live in peace. I heard from Trudy from time to time after she'd gone home and there was no chance of him eavesdropping on her conversation. She told me that Frank had taken to drinking heavily and that more strange men came to the house. They would meet behind closed doors. She also said Frank did a lot of traveling for business—crooked business, I suspect.

"It had been three years since I left Bradleyville, and I was only beginning to feel safe when one day after grocery shopping, there he was in the parking lot. He wasn't alone. There were two other men with him. I just knew that was it. He would haul me off to the woods and kill me. I was scared.

"He said, 'I have a proposition for you. You come back and give me a child, and then you can come and go as you please, if you leave for good by the time the child is three. That way, it won't really remember you. I'll give you a divorce, and you will sign a paper as soon as you become pregnant that you relinquish full custody to me. I'll never bother you again.'

I asked, 'Why on earth would I do that?' He answered, 'Because if you don't, I'll have your precious Sam killed and frame you for the murder. Then that bastard child of yours will go to the state children's home. You remember how good I am at framing people, don't you? I have connections all over the country and trust me I will do it.' I knew he would, and he would get away with it, just as he had gotten away with putting Sam in prison. Again, I did what I thought I had to, to protect my family that I loved.

"He had me send Sam a wire letting him know I had decided to go back to my husband where I belonged and for him not to come for me. I got pregnant right away, and it was not an easy pregnancy. The doctor confined me to bed for the last six months. Then Donna was born, the prettiest little girl in the world. There was no way I could ever leave her with him. But there was you and Sam, who I loved with all my heart.

"It was amazing the effect that Donna had on Frank. He was almost human and so tender with her. I believe if he was capable of love that he did love her. I was still weak for a long time after Donna was born. I had pneumonia in the hospital. I begged Trudy to see Sam and tell him the truth and that as soon as I was able, I would be with him and our son. I said, 'Tell them I love them and want to come home if they will have me. Please tell him not to come for me. That would not only be dangerous for him and Jimmy, but for the baby and me.' Trudy did as I asked her to. She said Sam promised her he would wait until he heard from me, but he made her promise if she saw any signs of violence from Frank to call him at once. Frank wouldn't let anyone but himself take care of Donna. He had confined his business to what he could tend to from home.

"When I was well enough to care for the baby, I told him there was no way I could leave my daughter. He thought I had decided to stay with him. He started toward me with a smile on his face, saying, 'I'm glad you have come to your senses.' I said, 'No, Frank, I mean I will be taking her with me.' He responded, 'May I remind you of the paper you signed when you first got pregnant? Should anything happen to end our marriage, you gave me full and complete custody of our child. You have three years to visit with both of your children. You can live with your lover, and I could care less anymore. I have what I want now, and I've grown tired of you. At the end of that time, I promise you, you will be leaving here alone and divorced, never to return.'

"My dear friend Trudy died that winter of a heart attack. I did not realize how much she had meant to me. I would miss her so very much. I lived in that hell for two years, hoping that one of his so-called business partners would turn on him and kill him. May God forgive me for my thoughts. I tried to come up with a plan to no avail. I was summoned to court at the end of three years for the divorce hearing. In the court-room, the Andersons swore under oath that I was a drug addict and an alcoholic. They also swore that I was abusive to Donna and would just go off and leave without notice and leave her alone.

"The judge granted the divorce and awarded Frank full custody of the child. It had also been determined that I would have no contact with her for her own good. Her father could more than amply support her and give her everything she would need. Defeated and heartbroken, I left Bradleyville.

"It was soon after that your daddy got so sick. He was the finest man I had ever known, and we loved each other enough not to dwell on the past. We finally decided it was time we got married, and we did, right here in this house. Sam was too weak for the ceremony. We did not need all that formal hoopla. All we had ever wanted was to be with each other.

"He surprised me with the same ring he had given me all those years ago. I thought after I had sold it to help with his defense that I would never see it again. To this day I do not know how he managed to get it back. I did sneak back from time to time without anyone knowing, to see Donna. I'd watch her from a distance while she played in the schoolyard. Then as she grew, I'd see her walking home from school with her friends. Dawn, it was probably you. She seemed happy. I even saw Frank and her together once. I must say, they looked devoted to each other.

"I could not shake her world. It would have been selfish and would have only caused her pain. I decided without delay not to go back again for fear I'd be spotted. I had you and your daddy to devote my time and love to, and you both needed me. I remember her in my prayers daily, and I'll never stop loving her."

Jessie was emotionally drained.

Jimmy said, "Mom, you've gone through enough."

"No, Jimmy, I want to finish. I hope the two of you won't judge me too harshly. I did what I thought I had to do to protect those I love."

We were both absolutely stunned at this horrific story. The pain and heartache she had been through in her life made me feel sick. This man that I had known all my life was a monster.

Jimmy said, "Mom, I am so sorry for the pain you have suffered. No one had better judge you in my presence. You did what you had to do at the time, not only for yourself but for your children."

I said, "Jessie, let me get you some tea."

"Thank you, Dawn. I'd like that."

Jimmy came into the kitchen to help me, and Jessie just sat looking out the window.

"Jimmy, does your mother know that Donna lives with me and Patsey?"

"Yes, I told her before I came out to get you."

"Now what do we do?"

"I think it is best to stay with Mom tonight. I do not want her to be alone. I cannot imagine a man who would treat other human beings like Frank MacIntosh did."

Leaving the kitchen, Jimmy said, "Mom, I know you must have questions about your daughter, and who better to answer your questions than her best friend? Dawn and Donna have known each other all their lives."

"I'd be happy to tell you about Donna, Jessie."

"I would like to know if she's been happy?" Jessie asked.

"She's been happy most of the time, but she has missed having a mother. She sort of adopted my mom as a substitute. I guess Jimmy already told you that she keeps a picture of you on the nightstand. Donna had gotten to the point that she constantly asked her dad about her mother. She always felt incomplete not knowing her mother. Frank finally gave her the picture of you. I know it's hard to believe, but he has always treated Donna like a princess. He has always worked a lot, so when she would get lonely, she'd just come stay with my family. She's an incredibly good person. She is a lot like her mother. She does volunteer work. She absolutely adores kids. Oh! I forgot, she just got engaged to a great guy, and they plan to be married soon. Donna does not want to wait, but Frank is trying to be sensible. I just realized he has the same first name as her father. That's weird; I never thought of that until now. You should know that she has been talking about trying to find you.

She has never seemed bitter toward you. She just gets sad sometimes because she never knew her mother."

Jessie sighed, "I feel better knowing she's had a good life. I have missed so much, and I would very much like to know this young woman, my daughter. I would never want to hurt her any more than I already have."

"I've got to ask you something, and I hope you don't think I'm prying, but aren't you afraid for her dad to know where you are?"

"Yes, I am smart enough to still be afraid of him."

"Jimmy, what do you think?" asked Dawn

"He could be dangerous still. I think we could all use a snack and some sleep before we decide what the next step should be. What do you think, Mom?"

"I think you're a pretty smart boy."

"Jessie, let me go in and heat up our leftovers from lunch, and you can freshen up and relax for a while, okay?" Dawn suggested.

"You are a sweet girl. I'm glad both of my children have you in their lives." She bent down and kissed Dawn's cheek.

"Mom, you don't have any doubts about how I feel about you, do you?" Jimmy asked.

Jessie just shook her head as if she was bewildered.

He went on, "I've got to tell you, if anything, all this has answered a lot of questions that I've had all my life. I always felt that somehow, when you were gone all those times, it was in some way my fault. I'm sure you already know how very much Daddy loved you, but I don't know if you knew what he was like when you were away. I would sometimes whine and complain because I wanted you here with me, He would take hold of my hands and lovingly look into my eyes and tell me not to be sad. He would say, 'Your mommy loves us. Just look forward to the time when she comes home, and we are all together again. Cherish those times, Jimmy. They are precious. One day when you grow up, my dream for you is that you find someone to love as much as I love your mother.'

Jessie had tears in her eyes, but her face had softened as she remembered this man who had been so devoted to her. The man had accepted her without question.

"Some may have thought he was weak and felt he should have gone to Frank himself, but I had asked him not to. I asked him to trust in my judgment and to wait for me. I know he wanted to go and kill Frank if necessary, anything to get him out of our lives for good, but he didn't. He and I both were afraid of Frank's power, and we knew he had the capabilities to cause us even longer lasting pain than he did. It is so easy for outsiders to say what they would have done, but we made our decisions together out of our love for each other and for you. Sam's only real regret was that I had to lose my child. He would have taken her in and loved her as his own daughter. I look back now, and I still can't produce a solution to the problems we faced back then. I don't know. I just don't know."

"Hey, we three had some great times together. Even after Daddy got sick; we had each other."

"We did what dad told us to do—we cherished our times together!"

Dawn said, "Okay, you two, soups on. Come and get it."

"Dawn, this is just what we need. I must tell you something. Even though it was a little like reliving the past all over again, I feel as though a giant load has been lifted from me, and just the possibility of one day getting to know my daughter is lifting my spirits."

"I should call Patsey and Donna and let them know I'm staying over."

Jimmy said, "I'm glad you mentioned that. I must call Professor Higgins and make sure he can teach my class tomorrow."

"You go first, Jimmy. I'm sure the girls stay up later than Dr. Higgins." We had to use the landline because service was weak.

After making the call, Jimmy said, "Okay, Professor Higgins will handle my classes, so I'm all set. Your turn, Dawn."

I could tell at once that something was wrong when Patsey answered the phone; her usually upbeat voice was very serious.

"Hey, girl," Dawn said. "What's up?"

"Oh, Dawn, am I glad you called. Are you all on your way?"

"No, we are still at Jessie's. What's wrong?"

"Well, it's been quite a day here. It's Donna's father!"

Patsey proceeded to tell me all that had happened. I could hardly believe what I was hearing, but after everything else I'd learned over the last few days, nothing should shock me.

When I could finally speak, I asked "How's Donna?"

"She's just been a mess. She was bordering on hysteria, but Frank got his doctor to phone in a sedative, so she is resting right now. She needs you here, though. I know it would be a big help."

"Okay, Patsey, I'll get there just as soon as I can. I'll see you in a little while."

When I hung up the phone, both Jimmy and Jessie were anxiously looking at me.

"Jimmy, Jessie, I am so sorry, but I must get home. Donna needs me." Jessie immediately asked,

"Dawn, what's wrong? Has Donna been hurt, or is she sick or something?"

"She's hurting, and I'm sure she is sick. Her father, Frank MacIntosh, was murdered today!"

"Oh my god! Donna must be devastated. If you two don't mind, I'd like to go," Jessie said. "I will just stay at your apartment, Jimmy. I won't intrude—I just want to be close by. Do you think that would be okay?"

"Sure, Mom. I don't like the idea of leaving you alone anyway. I'm not sure what to do about you and Donna, but we can worry about that later."

As I gathered my things together, I thought back over all that had happened to me since I had left home for college. Meeting Patsey and Jimmy by chance, learning so much about a man I thought I knew, and now this. It was just too much!

"Mom, if it's okay with you, we'll need to take your car. I don't think we'd all fit in the Vette."

"Sure. Here's my bag. I'm all set. I called Tommy Henderson, and he's gonna watch over the farm for me. I gave him your phone number in case he needs me."

Everybody seemed tense on the ride home. Finally, Jessie broke the silence.

"Did Patsey say if they knew who had murdered Frank?"

"Yes, it was Dan Anderson. The police are holding him in New York. That's where it happened. It seems that Mr. MacIntosh didn't die right away and was able to give the police quite a bit of information. He also dictated a letter for Donna, and the police will be bringing it as soon as it is released."

"How's Donna?"

"Frank gave her a sedative, and she's resting. In the morning, this is going to hit her like a ton of bricks."

I had Jimmy and Jessie drop me at the house. I decided the fewer people around right now, the better. Patsey greeted me at the door.

"Boy, I am glad you're home."

CHAPTER 15

"How's Donna?"

"She is asleep right now. Poor Frank is asleep in the rocker. I told him to get in a bed and I would let him know when Donna woke up, but he wouldn't leave her side. I am glad he has been here, though."

"How are you holding up, Patsey? You look pretty tired yourself."

"Oh, I'm fine. I'm just not particularly good at dealing with death. I guess Jimmy went on home?"

"Yeah, I thought it would be best. I'm going to peek in on Donna."

When I opened the door, I could see Frank sound asleep in the rocker, but I couldn't tell if Donna was asleep or not. When I turned to leave the room, I heard a small voice like a child's call my name.

"Please don't go. I'm not sleeping."

I went to her side, and Donna held on to me. I could feel her body shaking.

"Donna, I'm so sorry I wasn't here for you."

"Dawn, I just can't believe that Daddy is dead. I keep thinking I'll wake up in the morning and this will have all been a bad nightmare.

You know, I know it would hurt no matter what, but, Dawn, he was murdered, and by someone I thought was his friend."

"I'm in shock too. Listen, we will handle this together, and you have Frank, who loves you. Look at him. Patsey said he refused to leave your side."

Donna looked over, and with tears running down her cheeks, she forced a smile.

"Dawn, I know I have Frank, but I need you for this too."

"You've got me. Anything I can do to make this easier for you, I will do. I'll bet you haven't eaten anything. How about if I bring some food up for you?"

"I think I'd like to go down to the kitchen with you. I'll have some tea and something to eat, I promise."

Frank roused a little, and Donna got him to get in the bed, assuring him she would be fine.

Patsey hustled around getting tea and heating up Donna's favorite coffee cake.

"I know you guys probably need some privacy, so I can go upstairs," Patsey said.

"Don't you be silly. Like it or not, you're family now, and I need both of you," Donna told her.

We all cried and ate coffee cake, and it seemed, at least for a little while, everything was back to normal. Somebodies cell phone rang, and we all jumped and then just stared at the phone as if it was the enemy. It was Donna's.

I finally answered it.

The voice on the other end said, "Hello, is this Ms. MacIntosh?"

"No, this is her friend, could I help you?"

"I guess so. This is Sheriff Hackney. We have just received the letter from Ms. Macintosh's father, and we needed to know if she wanted it brought over tonight or in the morning."

"Let me ask Donna. Could you hold on for a moment?"

"Certainly, I can."

"Donna, they need to know if you want them to bring the letter from your dad tonight or in the morning."

"I want to see it tonight, as soon as possible. I need some answers."

I relayed the message, and then we waited.

After what seemed an eternity, the doorbell rang. The officer had to hand the letter over to Donna herself. She opened it and then just stood still.

"Do you want to be alone?" Dawn asked.

"No. If you don't mind, I can't be alone right now. Just give me a minute." As she read the letter, the tears started again, and then what looked like total shock and amazement came over her expression. Patsey and I sat and looked at her as if she were a volcano about to erupt. I kept wondering how much Frank MacIntosh had confessed in this letter if anything. He must have divulged something because Donna was as white as a sheet.

"This is unbelievable!" Donna exclaimed.

"I thought I knew my father, but I didn't know him at all. He was a crook, he cheated companies and people out of their money and their property, and he cheated me out of a mother. I don't know how to feel anymore. He got killed because he and Dan Anderson got involved with some people that pushed back, and my father was trying to leave the country with the money when Dan stopped him. Inside this other envelope is the name and address of my mother. My father even black-mailed her into leaving us so he wouldn't have to share me with her. That's not the worst of it—he knew she was in love with someone else, and he had manipulated her from the first time they met. He started making her life a living hell right from the start. He didn't leave her a choice. After I was born, he forced her to leave and never come back." Donna sat with the envelope clutched in her hand.

Suddenly, I didn't know what to do. Should I tell her or just let her read it? I would have to tell her what I had found out and how it had happened.

"Donna, before you finish that letter, I must tell you something." Then I stopped. My mind had gone blank.

"What did you want to tell me?"

"I know who your mother is. I just found out today."

"How could you know?"

"It's a long story, but it all started to fall into place the night of our party."

Donna looked totally confused, and who could blame her? I sounded like a blithering idiot.

"I think you should finish the letter, and then I'll try to fill in the missing pieces."

"I've waited for this information all of my life, and now I'm having a hard time reading this." She started reading again and then looked first at me, then at Patsey, and then she put the paper down on the table right in front of me. I saw Jessie's name and address.

"Donna, Jimmy is your brother. When I was showing him the house, he saw that picture you keep on your nightstand. He has one just like it. He never knew his mother had another child. Then he started to put the pieces together, and when we went to his mom's today, we learned the whole story from Jessie."

I thought Patsey was going to fall out of her chair. "You both may be mad at me for what I did, but last night after you and Frank went out, I went in to look at the picture. Since all of this crap from the party started over Jimmy seeing that picture, I was curious. I looked at it and saw Aunt Jessie I have felt so uneasy."

"Don't be silly, I would have done the same, if it had been me," Donna replied.

We all just sat as if in a trance.

"What's she like?" Donna asked.

"She's great, Donna. You will love her. She already loves you and always has. She is afraid you'll hate her and think she didn't try hard enough to keep you."

"Well, she never tried to contact me in all these years."

"I know, but—Donna, I do not want to hurt you or speak badly of your dad, but he made it impossible for her. Believe me, she has suffered as much as you have, more because she was forced to give up her child, a child she had given birth to and cared for and loved for three years. For years after she was forced out of your life, she would sneak around and watch you from afar. She said you seemed happy, and she could tell you adored your father and that he adored you. She said she thinks you were the only person in the entire world that he had ever loved. Donna, no matter what you find out in the days ahead, you need to remember that. Your dad did love you as best he could."

"I know that Daddy loved me, and damn it, I loved him. I just feel like I never knew him. All these years, my mother was so close, and I have a brother. This is more than I can understand."

"Well, I have one more thing to tell you. Your mother is right here in town. She rode back with Jimmy and me, and she is at Jimmy's apartment. She was worried about you, but she didn't think you needed any more to deal with right now."

Then Patsey spoke up. "We are family. You're my cousin."

At that, we all had to laugh. Frank walked into the kitchen, bleary-eyed and looking as if we had all lost control. Of course, we had, but considering all that had happened today, we were doing pretty well.

———//———

CHAPTER 16

Donna decided she needed to deal with the arrangements for her dad and get through settling his affairs before she could move on to anything else. The next week was spent handling business matters and planning the funeral.

As if things were not hard enough, the papers were riddled with stories about Frank MacIntosh and his life of crime. The day came for us to travel back to Bradleyville for the funeral. I had wanted to go back home for a visit, but not under these circumstances. I had called Mom and Daddy, to briefly fill them in. They hadn't known Donna's mother. They had only heard the town gossip, which hadn't even been close to the truth. Donna had asked that Jessie and Jimmy wait until she had dealt with the ordeal of the funeral before they got together. Mom had insisted that we all stay at our house, and Donna was relieved not to have to stay in her dad's house, at least not now.

Donna and Frank dropped me at my parents so I could have some time alone with them before the service. They had some last-minute business to attend to. When I walked in, there was no one to be found, and I just walked through the house and soaked in all the things in that house that were so much a part of who I was. I felt thankful for the kind of family I had. You never fully appreciate your family.

"Dawn! You're here." Whitney nearly knocked me over with a hug. Then Mom and Dad joined us.

"How long have you been here?" Whitney asked?

"Maybe the better question is, when did you get here and what's going on in London?" asked Dawn. "Where were the three of you?"

Then they all had a big group hug. Crying and laughing all at once.

"Out at the barn. One of the cows was having a tough time giving birth to her calf."

"Is everything okay?" Dawn asked.

"Yeah, Daddy helped her. She'll be fine. Where are Donna and Frank?"

"They had some things to take care of. They'll meet us at the church." said Whitney

"How's she doing?" Mom wondered.

"She's doing pretty good, considering all she's had to deal with in the last few days." Dawn answered.

"Did Jimmy and Jessie come?" Mom wondered.

"No, Donna thought it would be easier to wait until after the funeral to meet her mother. Even though her dad turned out to be such a creep, she loved him and felt she owed him this."

Daddy said, "I've got to tell you, I'm still in shock. I don't know why, but I always felt there was something fishy about Frank MacIntosh. I never said anything because we were so crazy about Donna, and I would never want to hurt her."

"Oh, Daddy, I'm so glad you're my dad." Well, thanks, honey. I think you've been just a little homesick."

"I guess so."

Then Whitney spoke up, "I'm glad you're my daddy too, and I've been a little homesick, if anyone cares," then altogether we grabbed hold of Whitney and said, "we all care."

"We'd all better get a move on it," said Mom. "You two girls go ahead and shower and change first. I'm gonna kick your dad and his muddy boots out the back door to get rid of a pound or two of dirt before he comes back in."

"Okay, Ida, I can take a hint."

As the two girls ran up the stairs talking ninety miles an hour, the two parents looked at each other and smiled a smile of pure contentment.

"Ida let's enjoy these two days with our girls home together. You never know when we'll all be together again."

"I know it's a sad event, but I agree with you, Bob."

"Well, are you gonna tell me about this hunk who has turned out to be Donna's brother, and just what does he mean to my big sister? Come on, give me the scoop." taunted Whitney

"Always the journalist, huh, scoop!"

"Do you want me to beat you up, or are you gonna talk?"

"Okay, don't get your underwear bunched up, first tell me why you didn't tell me you were coming home? How long are you home for? Where's Mary? asked Dawn.

"Okay, I'm here for two days, because, Mary sent me to gather some information from a few people near here, Mary is in London, so I took the opportunity to visit Mom and Dad, and before you explode,

I didn't know until the last minute. I didn't even tell them. You should have seen their faces. Then they told me about all of this drama. I haven't had two minutes to call anyone! Now it's your turn, we don't have much tine so, tell me about your man."

"Jimmy is very much like Donna. He's so easy to talk to. He really listens. He's a very dedicated instructor. He believes he can help people's quality of life with his knowledge of the land. He and Daddy should get along great. He's a simple man in many ways." Dawn said dreamily.

"Okay, cut to the chase. What does he look like?" Whitney asked.

"Oh, Whitney, I have missed you. He has black hair that shines like satin and brown eyes you can get lost in. He's six foot two, and has a great body, coming and going. He's not a pretty boy. His face has character, rugged looking, and he looks like a real outdoor man. He has the hands of a worker and the brain of a scholar."

"Oh, my god, you're hooked!" Whitney proclaimed.

"I'm not hooked, but I am 100 percent in love with this gentle, gorgeous man. Another thing that I like about him is how devoted he is to his mother. It helps me to know how he will treat the women in his life."

"I can't believe I'm not going to get to meet this perfect male specimen before I leave for England. I was hoping he would come with you, but I guess it would have been awkward. Mom's worried that you'll get married, have kids, and end up a farmer's wife."

"Oh, Whitney, we haven't been together long enough to make those decisions. Besides, he is in line for a grant that could take him out of the country for research. He's worked long and hard for that, and I would never stand in the way of him achieving his dreams." Dawn said.

"You're a better woman than I." Whitney said sexily.

"Hey, we've gotta get dressed. We can't be late. Donna needs to be there before anyone else arrives, "Dawn said.

Mom, Dad, and Whitney spoke to Donna about how badly they felt for her. She knew that their feelings came from the heart because they thought of her as another daughter. Frank talked with Pastor Michaels and then came over to us. Donna introduced him to all, and he said, "Pastor Michaels was wondering if it would be okay to get started."

"Sure, I think everyone who counts is here."

The truth was, besides the MacIntosh family lawyer and Frank MacIntosh's secretary, we were the only ones there. Then, Donna noticed another lady in the back.

This was a lady she didn't recognize, so before they started the service, she went to her and said, "I don't believe I know you."

The lady smiled at her and said she was Trudy's daughter, Hope. She had a letter her mother had given to her before she passed. "The letter was for you. She didn't want you to have it until your father was no longer a threat to anyone."

Donna took the letter to read at the end of the service.

The service was relatively short. No one got up to speak about Frank MacIntosh.

Dawn pondered, I guess that shows that his life had been self-centered, except for Donna. I guess all that money couldn't buy friends. No kind words or tears, from the few gathered.

As Donna opened the letter, she read the words Trudy had written. She read the letter carefully. She got to the part where Trudy mentioned that her dad had always treated her fairly, both as her boss and financially. She said that she couldn't face God unless she revealed to Donna who her real mother was. She asked forgiveness from Donna for keeping this secret for so long.

Your real mother was a good woman and a very loving mother. Her name is Jessie McCoy. Jessie contacted me often about your welfare.

Trudy went on to reveal all the sordid details that she knew about the forced marriage of Mr. MacIntosh and Jessie. Donna read the rest of the letter and then looked up at Hope.

"You do not know how happy I am that you came and shared this with me. You have helped me more than you will ever know. You remind me so much of Trudy. I hope we can stay connected."

Frank MacIntosh was buried in the only cemetery in Bradleyville. He had a family plot and had even made the arrangements for the headstone. He had asked that the only inscription be "Loving Father." He was finally put to rest, for the last time!

Back at Mom and Dad's, Mom took control. This was her domain. "You people just go on out of my kitchen and I'll have food on the table in no time flat. Dawn, get that pitcher of lemonade out of the fridge."

Whitney had packing to do, and Daddy asked Frank if he'd like to change into some jeans and ride the property with him. Frank hesitated to leave Donna, but she insisted.

Donna and I went up to my room to change. She asked me if I'd walk with her over to her house.

"Are you sure you're ready for that?"

"Yes, I'm ready to get on with my life. I do not think my father should be able to ruin even a day of anyone else's life. Dawn, my father didn't have any friends, not one. I don't want to end up like that."

We walked down the sidewalk, passing the neighborhood where we played and laughed with all the other kids. There were some neighbors outside, but they seemed to be pretending not to notice us.

All except one, old lady Elrod, who called us. She was planted out on her porch in a wheelchair. Mom had told me that she had taken to falling a lot, and the doctor thought it necessary. She also had a full-time nurse now. She beckoned us to come up to her. I remember thinking she was at least a hundred when I was a kid. This was the same woman we'd been scared of. Every time a ball or Frisbee would accidentally go into her yard, no one wanted to get it because she would stand on the porch, waving her cane and yelling, "Don't you kids trample my flower beds, or I'll have your heads!" Donna and I both looked at each other. What did she want with us?

We walked up to her, and she motioned for us to sit in the swing by her.

"Girls, just relax. I have something for you." She reached down into a big carpet bag that sat beside her chair. She pulled out a large photo album and handed it to us. To our surprise, it was filled with pictures of all the neighborhood kids. Many had come and gone over the years, but in every picture were Donna, Whitney, and I. It was like a testimony to our childhood.

Mrs. Elrod looked at us, a little teary-eyed, and said, "I know you kids didn't like me much, and who could blame you? I was an angry old woman. In my younger years, my husband and little girl both died in a tornado. It destroyed many homes and took the lives of twenty-three people in Bradleyville. I was so angry that I had lived, and my Otto and Angela had been taken from me. I watched you girls run and play, and I took pictures. You never noticed. You were too busy having fun. The pictures seemed to take the place of the family I had lost. I kept everyone at a distance for fear of losing anyone close to me again. I'm ninety-six now, and I want you to know how much joy watching you grow has brought me. I feel as though you were all mine, in a way. I only wish I'd had the courage to have you all in for cookies or to just sit and talk. Somethings you just do not learn until the moment has passed you by. I want you girls to have this and share it with the others whenever you have the chance."

"Are you sure you don't want to keep this?"

"No, I want you two to oversee it now. Donna, dear, I know you are going through some sad times, and I'm so sorry about that, but from time to time, just look through the album and remember the carefree times of your childhood. The freedom, laughter, and pure joy of being alive. Now come over here and give me a hug and be on your way. I know you have things to do."

As Donna and I walked away, we had a new understanding of more than just old Mrs. Elrod.

"I can't believe what just happened. It's so strange. If people could only know the truth before they decide to judge others—I don't know. I'm sure I've done it too, but it's just too bad. I know I'm rambling. Well, here we are. "Donna said.

We opened the door and right there to greet us was Clara, the house-keeper who had taken over the household duties when Trudy died.

"Oh, Ms. Donna, I'm so happy to see you. How are you? I was hoping you'd be staying here, but I know it's too hard right now. I hope you know that I would have been at the funeral, but we had workers here to repair a leak on the roof, and we have waited for two months for them to come. I did not want to miss them. These repairmen are in such demand, they have more work than they can handle."

"That's okay, Clara. I understand. Clara, I hope you can stay on, but I'm afraid I'll only need you part time."

"I didn't expect you would need ne as much but that fits right in with my plans. I've been wanting to cut my hours down anyway. Can I get the two of you anything?"

"No thanks, Clara. We're just gonna poke around. Dawn, what would you think of me redoing this whole house?"

"Are you and Frank planning on living here after you're married?"

"Yes, we talked about it and decided we want to live here n Bradleyville. Frank is going to take over Daddy's law practice and run the office. He did have several legitimate clients. I want it to be more my style, homier."

"Are you gonna have time to do all of this and still handle School?" asked Dawn.

"No, I've decided to quit school. I certainly don't need to work. Even after I make restitution to all the people my father owed money to, I'll still have plenty. You know, that's what really bothers me. He could have made a great living with his law practice and stayed honest. Anyway, you know all I ever wanted to do was be a wife and mother. Frank and I are getting married sooner than we had planned. He can do his intern work right here with the senior attorney at the firm."

"How does Frank feel about taking on the responsibility of a law practice?"

"He's a bit overwhelmed, but he wants to at least try. Besides, I want some free time to get to know my mother and my brother. By the way, have you met my brother?" Donna asked.

"Very funny!" replied Dawn.

"Don't worry, I'm not going to desert you and Patsey. I insist on still putting in my third of the expenses." Donna said,

"That's silly, you don't have to do that"

"I know I don't have to, but I want to. Besides, I will still be visiting my two best friends. There is one thing you could do for me."

"Sure, anything."

"I wondered if you would call my mother and Jimmy and see if they could come over to our house Sunday afternoon. We should be home around one, so any time after that would be fine."

"No problem. I'll take care of it."

It was an emotional goodbye since I knew I wouldn't be seeing Whitney for such a long time. She would be flying back to England in two days to her new life. I looked back at her as we were leaving. She would be different the next time I saw her.

"Oh, Dawn, Whitney will always be our little sister," Donna said.

—#—

CHAPTER 17

I had called Jessie and Jimmy, and they were more than happy to come over. I also called Patsey to fill her in on the coming events. She informed me that she would cook a big Sunday dinner, complete with my favorite pie. I scolded her for doing so much, but she said that's how she handles stress.

I could smell the wonderful smells from the kitchen even before we opened the door.

"Would you just look at this place. You have been busy, haven't you?" Donna said.

"Donna, I want you to know my heart was with you today. I'm just not good at those kinds of things. When Dawn called and said you wanted her and I to come for dinner also, I was thinking, we are family now, you're my cousin." Patsey said.

Donna responded, "I couldn't be happier to be in your family" they hugged.

The doorbell rang, and Donna was on her feet, looking like a nervous cat. Patsey opened the door to Jessie and Jimmy.

Patsey greeted them, "Aunt Jessie, it's great to see you. You too, Jimmy. Come on in. Everyone's in the living room."

When Jessie walked into the living room, both she and Donna had the same reaction. They stood for a minute just looking at each other, smiling with tears rolling down their cheeks.

"My dear, sweet daughter, I've waited for this day for so many years."

Then they fell into each other's arms.

"Oh, Mama. I can't believe it. I finally have a mother."

The entire room was filled with such love that it was a bit overwhelming. Jimmy held onto my hand so tightly that it nearly broke.

Jessie took Donna over to Jimmy. "I know you two have met, but not as sister and brother." She took both their hands and stood before them. "God, thank you for this day with my two children."

Donna walked over and picked up a large book and gave it to Jessie. "This is a present for you. It's an album full of my childhood pictures. I thought you should have it."

"Oh, Donna, I will treasure this always."

The day was filled with lots of catching up, eating, and laughing. Donna announced to Jimmy that she had a present for him also. She was donating the money to the university so that his project would be approved. Jimmy jumped up and gave Donna the biggest hug, and just kept thanking her.

Donna wasn't going to tell him, but she wanted to see the relief on his face, when he knew, it was really going to happen.

CHAPTER 18

In the weeks ahead, we all tried to get our lives back to a normal routine. Donna went in to withdraw from school and was talked into taking the rest of her schooling by computer. It turned out to be great for her. She worked out a combination schedule where she did some of her hours on the computer and her exams and some hours of classroom work at the university. I felt better that she was at least going to continue in some way. Frank felt better about this arrangement, and he said it would give Donna the chance to spend time with Patsey and me.

Donna and Jessie were thick as thieves. They spent every opportunity to make up for lost time. Jimmy and I didn't see much of each other for a couple of weeks. I had exams and makeup work. I was so stressed. I was beginning to be envious of Donna's new arrangement. Jimmy was busy preparing for the upcoming adventure. He had meetings with the board of directors at the school. They interviewed ambassadors from several foreign countries. He was absolutely like a man possessed, but in a good way. He was so exhilarated.

I tried to equal his enthusiasm, but in the back of my mind, all I could think of was that this would be a two-year project with no breaks for trips home.

I was feeling sorry for myself. I had found love only to lose it, at least temporarily, and who knew? Two years can change a person a lot.

It had been exactly seven days since we'd seen each other. We'd talked on the phone, and I had listened to Jimmy go on and on about the progress of what I had begun to think of as the Project I'm Doing Something with My Life and You're Not!" I woke up in a major PMS mood. I had all the typical symptoms. I was bloated, cramping, and I fluctuated between bitching and crying. On top of everything else, I had a zit the size of a grapefruit on my chin. I didn't get out of my gown and robe all day. I ate everything that was sweet or fattening in the house.

At 3:00 p.m., I had piled myself up in bed with a bag of chips and a Coke and watched *A Love Affair*. Since I was wallowing in self-pity, I was talking back to the television: "Yeah, like that could happen." This movie that I had once found so tender and heartwarming was irritating the life out of me. At 3:45 p.m., the doorbell rang, and I debated whether to just ignore it or go down and dare whoever had dared darken my door to say one word about my appearance. I opted for the latter. I shuffled down in my slippers to the door.

I opened the door to a delivery man from the campus florist holding a large arrangement of blush roses, my favorite, and a card. It was a boy who looked too young to even be driving. He snippily commented that he was sorry to have gotten me out of bed. I thought, well, there goes your tip, friend.

"Ma'am, you forgot your card."

Who does he think he is calling ma'am, young punk! This should have lifted my spirits, but not today. I guess He's just too busy to come by in person. I took the card upstairs with me, plopped back down on my bed and opened it.

This is but a mere token of appreciation for your understanding, patience, and love. I have been so neglectful of you, and I'm hoping that you will let me start to make it up to you tonight. I will be over at seven to kidnap you for the entire weekend. Pack your bathing suit and your prettiest outfit. No one will be able to contact us because I'm not even telling you where we're going. If I don't hear from you by five, I will assume that you agree with my plans. I need to see your face and have you near me.

Love,
Jimmy

My heart began to soften, and excitement took the place of self-pity. I had a purpose now, at least for the day. I jumped in the shower, put about a pound of zit zapper on my chin, and tried to pack. Where would we be going, that I need my bathing suit? It was only about thirty degrees outside. I decided on a sleek little pants outfit I had just bought that made me look pretty sexy, if I did say so myself. I packed several other outfits, a dinner dress, and I paid particular attention to my lingerie. I was happy, I was excited, and I *was going out*!

Jimmy arrived promptly at seven, looking particularly handsome. He waved a white flag as I opened the door, which brought an instant smile to my face.

"Please say you still love me."

"I don't know. Are you going to disappear again if I tell you I still love you?"

"Dawn Prackett, you have a wicked streak in you. I think I could grow to like it. As much as I'd like to ravish your body right here and now, we must be on our way."

"Where might that be?" she asked.

"You'll see. Is this all of your luggage?"

As I was answering and walking out the door, I noticed a white limo at the curb with the driver standing beside it.

"What's going on?"

"Come on, my lady. Your carriage awaits."

Inside the limo was a single rose, a small, beautifully wrapped package, and champagne on ice. We pulled away from the curb and Jimmy handed me the rose and poured the champagne.

"Dawn, I know we haven't known each other long, but I believe in the great scheme of life, we were meant to find each other. It would make me the happiest, most fulfilled man in the world if you would agree to be my wife. To live together, love together, and grow old together."

"Oh, Jimmy, I can't think of anything that would make my life more complete."

Then he handed me the little package. It was the most beautiful ring. It had a diamond in the center and encircling that were eight smaller diamonds. The setting and band were antique.

"This ring belonged to my grandmother," Jimmy said. "It's not a big diamond, but it has always meant a lot to me."

"It's gorgeous. I will cherish it forever."

We fell into each other's arms, and when he kissed me, I knew that not even space or time could keep us from loving each other.

"Hey, are you going to tell me where you're taking me?"

"We're going to someplace carefree and sunny with white sandy beaches and crystal clear water as far as the eye can see. We're flying off to Jamaica."

"Oh, Jimmy, I can't believe it. I've been so cold and so miserable this week. I'm afraid I've been feeling sorry for myself." she said, with a pouty face.

"I know I've been so absorbed in my work that I neglected you, but, Dawn, I've gotta tell you, it is very important to me."

"I know, and I'm proud of you for that."

"I want you to know that you are the most important part of my life. Are you okay with me going away for so long? "Jimmy asked.

"Well, I will miss you with every fiber of my being, but I know how long you've dreamed of this opportunity. I'll tell you what—you show me this weekend just how much you'll miss me by ravishing my body."

"I think I can manage that just fine, but you might want to at least see the beach."

———#———

As we stepped off the plane in Jamaica, there was a group of locals playing steel drums, singing, and dancing. What a beautiful, playful place Jamaica was. Jimmy and I managed quite easily to adjust to the lifestyle. We had dinner out on our private terrace, which opened onto the beach. We could hear the waves rush in and roll away. What an incredibly tranquil sound that was. The exotic flowers that surrounded the grounds of our hotel were breathtaking both in their beauty and their scent. We could hear music.

"This is so beautiful. Let's never leave."

"Okay, but I hope you like coconuts and oranges, a lot, because as beach bums that will be our diet."

We decided to throw caution to the wind and wander down to the water, shed our clothes, and swim in the nude. This proved to be more than either of us could handle. Our naked bodies washed up onto the shore wrapped together, and we devoured each other right then and there.

We were brought back to earth by the sounds of approaching voices, so we wrapped our clothes around us and ran giggling to our room for a repeat performance. Our lovemaking was so natural, but at the same time, it was like the first time. The eagerness of our kisses and the passionate but sensitive touching aroused every part of me. The best part was that it touched and aroused me in a deeper part of my body—in my heart!

The next morning, I woke up, and Jimmy was already up. I could hear him in the bathroom. When he came out, I thought I'd burst from laughing. There he stood in his cowboy boots, and Speedo swimsuit, and his cowboy hat.

"Anyone for a swim?" He said with a grin on his face.

Dawn replied, through her laughter."

Of course I am, but not with you in that banana hammock."

"How do those guys go out in public in these?" He laughed along with me. "Lucky for you, I brought another suit."

"Oh darn. You mean all those native girls out there are going to be cheated out of that gorgeous body?"

"I'm afraid so but look in the bag by the bed. I hope it fits."

"It better have more cloth than that one does." Dawn added.

"It does. Haven't I ever told you how bad I am at sharing?"

Then there was a knock at the door —room service—and, We both laughed as Jimmy scrambled for his robe. After eating breakfast, Jimmy changed into a more proper pair of swim trunks, and we headed to the beach. It was so secluded. It was like our private beach, which was perfect.

The rest of our time was spent getting to know every aspect of each other. I had never known anyone with whom I could be so open and honest without fear of being judged or changed. We each knew neither one of us was perfect, but that was okay.

"Dawn, I hope you don't take this wrong, but I don't think I could ever be jealous over you. I mean, I almost feel bad for all those guys out there who'll never know the wonderful and sexy woman that you are. Seriously, I trust you with my heart and soul, and I want you to know that I value your trust in me."

"Jimmy, I feel the same way. I hope Donna and Frank will be as happy as we are."

"I like Frank. It's going to be nice having him as a brother-in-law."

"Donna and I always wanted to be sisters, and now at least we'll be sisters-in-law."

"I'm gonna miss this place, but I don't mind going home."

"I'll tell you what—we'll come here every year on our anniversary."

"That's a deal." Dawn said with a gleam in her eyes.

We haven't talked about when we want to get married, but, if it's okay, I'd rather wait until I return from my trip. I don't want to just marry you and leave. I want for us to have a wedding and a honeymoon, the whole thing. What do you think?"

"I think that would be best. I'd like for Whitney to be my maid of honor, and she's in England for quite some time. As a matter of fact, she should be coming back about the same time as you are."

I couldn't wait to tell my news to the girls and Mom and Dad, and I had to call Whitney. I didn't care if she was in England—I'd splurge.

———//———

CHAPTER 19

The next few months were pretty busy. Jimmy became a frequent overnight visitor. I guess we had gotten spoiled being around each other so much in Jamaica. Jimmy's plans for his project were coming along better than he'd hoped. The country had been chosen; it was Bosnia. The government felt it would be a great show of goodwill, and it would also be a challenging experience for Jimmy. These people could really use the help, and he was prepared to teach them. I was worried, though. It was, to say the least, an erratic country.

I only had him for another four months, and then he'd be gone for at least a year. The time had been shortened from two years to one with the possibility of a three-month extension. Jimmy agreed that this was a wise decision. Since Jimmy was going be away for so long, the college gave him the month before he left. This would allow him to be with his family. Donna, Patsey, Jessie, and I had decided it would be a great idea to have a McCoy/Connors family reunion before he left. It would also give Jessie a chance to introduce her daughter to her relatives. Donna and Frank had also moved their wedding plans up so that Jimmy could be here for it. Donna had asked my daddy to give her away, and he was so pleased. Whitney had hoped to come home for the wedding, but she and Mary already had schedules that couldn't be changed, as well as a trip to France that same week. She was so disappointed.

CHAPTER 20

Whitney explained to me a little about the importance of these interviews.

Mary and Whitney had several interviews with different contract companies who transported supplies and equipment as well as do building for the military. These companies had been working for the military during the Iraq War.

Mary said some were legitimate while others were not. When Mary did her articles, she didn't hide the truth. She got both sides of the story.

Whitney was a little nervous about the reluctance of the companies to speak to them. Mary had done all of the financial background on the companies, even the hidden financials, Whitney knew that Mary was experienced in dealing with things like this, but it was her first time.

Mary had told her that some of the things they had done caused fatalities not only to our military, but to innocent women and children, If Mary could stop this and bring the truth to light then the federal government could stop any more harm from happening then put these companies out of business and charged for murders.

Whitney thought if she truly wanted to be a journalist she needed to get in the right mind set and give these interviews her best shot. Even when there were eye witness accounts from US soldiers, the government is dragging their feet on prosecuting them. Yes, there is definitely a story that needs to be told to the American population.

Whitney had to admit that she had to be cautious about who knew what, until the book was released.

These incidents that she was gathering information on civilians and military fatalities, were from 2006.

The soldiers that were there haven't forgotten!

Another atrocity is that many of our brave soldiers from that war are suffering from PTSD or are homeless, after giving of their lives to help us.

Our vets are getting subpar treatment, while The U.S. Egypt Higher Education Initiative, has a $250 million investment to educate Egyptian students.

CHAPTER 21

The reunion was held at Jessie's farm. Donna had gone to stay with Jessie the whole week before to help her get things ready. Patsey even took a couple of days off work and school for the event. Her mom and dad were coming, of course. Jessie and Patsey's dad, were brother and sister. There were aunts and uncles and cousins by the dozens. Mom and Dad were invited.

The kids ran and played, and I sat back and marveled at how Great Jimmy was with them. You could tell he loved kids. This pleased me since someday I wanted to have a few of our own. Mom and Dad finally got to meet Jimmy. Mom was a little upset to think I was going to get married and settle for being a homemaker. Daddy was happy for us. He and Jimmy got along great right from the start, just like I knew they would.

Mom just needed some time, I hope.

Dad told me before they left that day that Jimmy had pulled him aside to ask for his blessing on our marriage. Dad had respected him for valuing some of the old-fashioned ways.

Jessie was such a proud mother. They all got together for the big family picture. There Donna was by her newfound mother and brother and all the rest of her new relatives. She had always wanted to be a part of a big family, and now she had one all of her own. She was absolutely glowing. It was a great day!

Now with the reunion behind us, it was on to completing the wedding plans. I was to be maid of honor, and Patsey was the only other bridesmaid. Donna had decided to have a very simple wedding with family and a few friends from school. She came to me and wondered if I thought my dad would mind if he didn't give her away.

"I mean, you know I love him, but I was thinking, there's no hard-and-fast rule that says a mother can't give a bride away, is there?"

"Oh, Donna, that's a great idea, and under the circumstances, Daddy will certainly understand."

"I'm gonna ask Mom tomorrow when I go see her. Would you mind terribly explaining things to your dad?"

"Sure, I will. Don't worry about anything. Jimmy said he's driving you to Jessie's, and the three of you are spending the weekend together," Dawn commented.

"Yes, I hate to take him away from you even for a few days, but I think it's important to Mom, and we don't want to disappoint her." Donna said pleadingly.

"Don't be silly," Dawn said.

The wedding was only a week away! Jessie was thrilled that Donna wanted her to give her away. The gown Donna had chosen was elegant yet very traditional. Reverend Michaels was going to perform the ceremony at Bonds Chapel in Bradleyville. Frank and Donna had decided on Jamaica for their honeymoon. After hearing how much Jimmy and

I had liked it, they thought it sounded perfect. Frank's parents were flying in, a few days ahead to meet Donna. She was a little nervous but too busy to dwell on it. My dress was beautiful. It was forest-green velvet, and Patsey's was also forest green but a little different.Both of us were to carry white fur muffs with a sprig of holly on them. Patsey's brother, Ronnie, had a little girl, Isabella, who was the flower girl, and she had a little dress the same design as Patsey's in a soft gold color.

The day of the wedding, Donna was sick all morning. We all thought she was just nervous and a bit run-down, but right before she was to walk down the aisle, she and I had a private talk.

"Dawn, I want you to know something. No one knows except Frank and Mama. "Donna said.

"Well, you certainly have my full attention. Nothing's wrong, is it?" Dawn asked.

"No, of course not. As a matter of fact, I couldn't be happier. I'm pregnant!" Donna said as she glowed.

Well, my mouth flew open. "That's why you're sick." Dawn sympathized.

"Yes, I've been a little sick to my stomach for a few weeks." Then Dawn asked,

"How far along are you?" I'm three months. Haven't you noticed this extra weight around my waist?" Donna said as she circled her tummy.

"No, but now that I think of it, you have been wearing a lot of loose clothes, but you're by no means big." Dawn replied.

"I will be very soon, I'm sure. My appetite is huge. Mom said she gained about twenty-five pounds when she was pregnant with me."

"I'm so happy for you. I know this makes everything complete for you. You will be a wonderful mother."

"Thank you for not saying all the typical things—you know, 'Well, I'm happy if you are' or 'That's all you need, a baby right away.' I know that most people wait until they're settled. I don't care what anyone thinks. We are so happy, and we're ready." Dawn smiled at Donna and said,

"That's all that matters. You better get going, best friend, or this baby won't be legal."

"I love you, and I 'm so glad I have you in my life, Dawn."

"You know I feel the same. Okay, let's get this wedding going! You are a beautiful bride."

The wedding was picture-perfect.

Jessie was so proud to be walking her daughter down the aisle. When the two of them reached the rest of the wedding party, Donna pulled a single white rose from the center of her bouquet and handed it to Jessie as she bent to kiss her cheek and squeeze her hand. At this point, there wasn't a dry eye in the house. They exchanged a special look, and both of them understood without words how happy they were to have finally found each other. Frank had asked his dad to be his best man. The vows were exchanged, and Pastor Michaels turned to the audience and announced, "May I introduce you all to Mr. and Mrs. Frank Kellums."

This was going be one of the good ones; this marriage was made of love. Frank was a good man. They each respected the others' opinion and feelings.

The reception was simple, not at all what you'd expect for someone of their financial standing. It was held on the grounds of the MacIntosh house, or should I say Donna and Frank's house. Oscar, the gardener, had all the flowers looking absolutely beautiful. It was a blending of family and friends, and surprisingly the media hadn't even bothered to crash the event for more gossip or pictures for the morning paper.

I was so pleased to see Hope, her husband, and darling little girl sitting toward the back of the church on the bride's side. I didn't know it at the time, but I later learned that Donna had set up a trust fund for Hope's daughter, out of gratitude for all Trudy had done for her as a child.Before we knew it, the happy couple was off to their two weeks in Jamaica. I must say I envied them that.

CHAPTER 22

Jimmy came up behind me and put his arms around me and said, "Why don't you go change and then let's take a walk?"

Okay, sounds good. I'll be right back."

As we walked through the old neighborhood holding hands, Jimmy caught me a bit off guard.

"I know after seeing this wedding, you might not be interested in what I'm about to say, but here goes. What would you think about becoming my wife before I leave for my trip? It wouldn't be a big fancy wedding, but we could do it all over again when I come home, and we could have any kind of wedding you want. I just really want us to get married as soon as possible and spend as much time together as we can."

Jimmy had not been looking at me as he spoke. If he had been, he would have seen that I had tears running down my face. He thought he had been insensitive to my feelings and that I was upset over him not wanting to wait for a wedding ceremony. He couldn't have been more wrong, and when I finally found my voice, I told him, "Jimmy, nothing would make me happier. I don't need the big ceremony. I do have one request: Could we at least have Reverend Michaels marry us at the church? We could have Jessie, Patsey, and Mom and Dad. It's important to me for us to say our vows in a church. Is that okay?"

"You bet.I already thought about that, and I agree. Let's go tell everyone, I think they are all at your mom and dad's house."

"Wait a minute, Jimmy, when do you want to do this?"

"Well," he stammered, "I was thinking' since we have everyone here that we could do it tomorrow. I already spoke to Reverend Michaels, and he said he had the church available at 5:00 p.m. We can get the wedding license in the morning anytime after 9:00 a.m."

"Okay. Let's get home. There are still a few things to take care of."

When we got to Mom and Dad's, everyone was sitting around the kitchen table, drinking coffee and talking about the day's events. They all looked when we came in, and Daddy said, "Hey, you two. I guess we'll be planning your wedding next."

Jimmy and I looked at each other and laughed.

"What are you two up to?"

"We were beginning to think that you two had gone with Donna and Frank."

"Actually, we have something to discuss with all of you." Jimmy replied.

Well, that statement quieted the room. We told them our plan. As with most families, we had those who weren't in complete agreement, but the general consensus was if it was what we wanted, then that's what we should do. The one who didn't seem too thrilled was Mom. While everyone else was hugging and getting caught up in the new excitement, she simply slipped out of the kitchen. Of course, I knew where to find her.

Jimmy had also picked up on the situation and looked at me in concern. I whispered to him that everything would be okay, and no one noticed when I left the room. They were too busy making plans for the next day's events. When I walked into the laundry room, there was Mom loading towels into the washer.

"Hi, honey. I just wanted to get these things done up before morning."

Sure, she did. For as long as I could remember, this was where Mom ran to when something was bothering her.

"Mom, please tell me what's bothering you."

When she turned and looked at me, there were tears in her eyes. It was one of the few times I'd ever seen my mother cry.

"You're not okay with us getting married, are you?"

"It's not exactly that. It's really just selfish. Since you were born, I've thought of the day you'd get married and what kind of wedding we'd be able to give you. Dawn, I know you've always been closer to your daddy, and that's okay, because the two of you are like two peas in a pod. I've always been the more practical one, and sometimes it makes me look a little cold and unfeeling, but I have only wanted the very best for you and your sister."

By now, I had tears in my eyes.

"Oh, sweetheart, don't cry. I can see that you and Jimmy love each other. It shows. It's just that marriage is hard at times, and to be left alone for at least a year or so...It's going to be extremely hard and lonely for you. Jimmy will be gone, Whitney is out of the country, and Donna has a new life of her own—I just worry about you."

I hugged her, and she held on tight. At that moment, I felt more love from my mother than I had in many years.

"Mother, I don't want to disappoint you or cause you worry, but I've waited for this day my whole life. I've always known there was that one true love out there waiting for me, and, Mama, Jimmy is my one true love. I could wait on him as long as it takes. Just knowing that he's mine and I'm his will get me through. Besides, I'll have you and Daddy and Jessie and Patsey. There's one more thing that you don't know. I don't want you to think any less of Donna, but she's pregnant, and she'll need her best friend around to help with the new baby."

At that moment, Jimmy peeked around the corner and saw us hugging and in tears.

"Ida, please don't be upset with Dawn. This was all my idea. I didn't mean to upset you or anyone."

Before he could go on, Mom walked over and gave him a hug and said, "Son, if my daughter is getting married tomorrow, we're gonna need some more coffee. We have plans to make!" She looked at both of us and smiled. "Just promise me one thing. Cherish the love that you have for each other, and don't ever be too comfortable to express it. That man in there probably doesn't know it, but he is and has always been my one true love. Now let's get busy."

Jimmy looked at us and took hold of my mom's hand and said, "Ida, I'm gonna like being part of this family."

We joined the others and drank what seemed like a gallon of coffee. Everyone was given their assignments. Jessie brought up the question of what Dawn planned to wear.

"I have absolutely no idea."

Mom looked at Daddy and then at me and said, "Now, only if you want to, but I do have something that you might like. Jim, could you get me the box from the cedar chest in our room?"

Daddy was beaming when he handed the box to Mom.

"Dawn, this was the dress I married your daddy in. If you don't like it, that's perfectly okay."

I opened the box, and the dress was the most breathtaking dress I had ever seen. It was antique white silk over satin with little pearl buttons on the sleeves and up the back. It wasn't the traditional lace and frills; it was simple and elegant.

"Oh, Mom, it's perfect."

Mom opened the neckline to reveal a small tag sewn into the dress. *This gown was made with love for my daughter.* It had Grandma's name on it: Margaret Ida Sellers.

Daddy took hold of Mom's hand and looked at her with such love. "Your mother was the prettiest bride I have ever seen."

He went into their room and brought out a picture from their bureau and showed us their wedding picture. There in the picture was a young couple full of hopes and dreams for the future. My mother's life may not have been as exciting as she had hoped, but I knew, then and there, she had no regrets.

"Is anybody hungry? Jesse and I can fix some supper."

Everyone was busy doing one thing or another except for Patsey and me. This was the perfect opportunity to ask her to be my maid of honor. She was thrilled, and we agreed she would wear the dress that she wore in Donna's wedding.

Jimmy had asked Daddy if he could be the best man and father of the bride. He beamed as he told Jimmy he was sure he could handle the dual role.

"You know, I've never really regretted not having a son, but I do think it's gonna be kind of nice to have one now. As a matter of fact, why not start now? How about helping me in the barn for a spell?"

"Sure thing, but do you think it's safe to leave these four women in here to their plans? We could come back to more jobs than even you and I can handle."

Daddy slapped him on the back and said, "You'll just have to get used to that, son."

Everything was falling into place, almost too perfectly. It was almost an intrusion in the plans when the phone rang. I picked it up, and it was Whitney on the other end.

"Hey there, I thought I'd catch you all there. I'll bet you're all sitting around the kitchen table yakking about the wedding."

"Well, you're partly right, but we're talking about my wedding."

"Hold on now. What are you talking about? You didn't go and get married too?"

"No, not yet, but we're gonna get married tomorrow."

"What? You can't get married without me."

I filled her in on all the details, and she was disappointed that she'd miss it, but she understood.

"I have a great idea. Ask Mom if there's a phone in the preacher's office just off the sanctuary."

Mom agreed that there was.

"Okay, tell me the number and what time, and I'll call. At least I'll get to hear it and be a part of it long-distance."

Mom gave her the number and thought it was a great idea, and we assured her that somebody would be taking some pictures.

Before long, we had done all we could do for the night, and it was time for some sleep. Just before I climbed the stairs to my old room, Jimmy said, "I can't believe it. Tomorrow you'll be Mrs. Jimmy Connors." He gave me a kiss goodnight.

The next morning, Jimmy and I got up early and were at the court house at the minute it opened. Then it was on to get our blood tests done at the hospital. When we came out the door, Daddy was waiting for us.

"Okay, you two. Don't you know it's bad luck to see the bride on her wedding day?"

"Hi, Daddy."

"Okay, I'm stealing this man from you for a while. You go home or do whatever you need to do the rest of the day. The next time you'll see him will be at the church."

"Jimmy, it doesn't sound like you have a choice. Don't you lose that license. See you two later."

When I got back, Mom, Jessie, and Patsey were laughing and talking as if they'd known each other all their lives. Mom was getting breakfast ready, and Jesse was baking a cake. I think it was our wedding cake because she shooed me away when I got too close. Patsey was washing dishes.

Mom asked where Jimmy and Daddy were?

"When Jim left, he said he was going into steal Jimmy away for the day, but he wouldn't say where he was going or what they were going to do. He did say they'd be back in plenty of time for the wedding."

Jim had taken Jimmy out to the woods on a narrow, winding road. It was so peaceful out there in the country. The wind was rustling through the leaves on the big maple and oak trees. The birds were chirping, and the squirrels were scampering along on the ground and up the trees. At the end of the road sat a small cottage. It had flower boxes at the front windows and a small front porch with two high-back rockers sitting on it. Hanging from the eaves was a hummingbird feeder. It was quite a modest little house, but it had charm.

"I didn't know you and Ida had another house on your property."

"Yeah, I built this little house with my dad just before I asked Ida to marry me. We lived here until the girls came along. Then about ten years ago, Ida's mom and dad decided they were getting too old to tend to their farm, and they lived here for about five years. Then they moved in with Ida's older sister, Francis, and her husband. Their health was failing, and Francis's kids were all grown. She and John had that big house that sits up on the hill behind the Methodist church. So, she wanted them with her to kind of fill up the emptiness since the kids were out on their own."

"Are they still living?"

"No, Grammy and Pop both died about two years ago. Pop had a heart attack in January, and Grammy died in April. I don't think she ever got used to being alone, living without Pop. They'd been married for seventy years."

"Did you need to do some work on the house?"

"Not exactly. Why?"

"Well, I thought maybe you needed me to help you with something."

"Oh, I forgot I hadn't told you why we were coming out here. I thought we'd air out the old cottage and make sure everything was in order, then maybe you two kids could spend your honeymoon out here. I know it's not fancy, but I also know you don't have the time to get away. I promise I won't let Ida come calling on you. There's no phone, but there should be everything else you might need."

"Jim, that sounds great. Let's have a look at it." After going inside, he said, "This is a great house. Everything is so clean. Hey, there's even a fireplace."

"It keeps most of the house warm enough, but there is a small space heater in the bedroom. Ida comes up here once a week and cleans and dusts. I think it makes her feel closer to her parents when she's here. I know Ida has clean sheets and towels, and the kitchen is all set up except stocking the refrigerator."

"Let's take a look around and see what else might need to be done."

"Son, the women are busy, so it's up to us to get things done here and go to the grocery."

After they'd stocked the wood pile enough to fill the wood boxes, they sat back and surveyed their handiwork.

"It may not pass Ida's seal of approval, but Donna will love it. Jimmy, I'm not a very educated man, and I'm okay with that. I've always worked hard at what I love, and I've been lucky in my life. I married a good woman who gave me two girls who have never disappointed me. Those women are my life, and it's not easy to hand one over. But

I know my Dawn, and I know her heart is set on you. I think you're a good and honest man and hope my questions won't make you mad, but I need to get them said. I need to know that you're gonna love my daughter in the hard times and that she's the one you want to look across the table at in fifty years and still want to hold her hand. That you'll find it hard to sleep unless her head is on the next pillow. That you'll feel sad when she's sad and feel joy when she feels joy. To know that you'll love her more with each passing year."

"Sam, I know what a special person Dawn is, and I already love her more with each passing day. I grew up in a family that taught me the value of love and family. I want to grow old together and to know the love of children and grandchildren. I only hope when the time comes to let one of my children go, I'll handle it as well as their grandpa did."

With that, they shook hands and went about their work.

—*//*—

I seemed to be in the way in the kitchen; no one would let me help. I flopped down on my bed, and it hit me: this is my wedding day!

I hoped I'd be a good wife. I didn't want to be one of those little simpering wives who cater to their husband's every whim. I want it to be give-and-take. I knew we'd have arguments and disappointments but that's just part of life. We need some bad times to make us appreciate the good times. I loved Jimmy, and he loved me, and that was all that mattered. Finally, I had time to read my letter from Whit.

Dear Sis,

Just wanted to let you know that I've met a new friend. Her name is Debbie Ray. She sets up computer systems for large companies. Her home base is here in London. One of her accounts is in the same building where mine and Mary's offices are located. We hit it off at once. Mary and I get along great, but there is quite an age difference, so having someone closer to my own age is fun to go out with and have girl talk. I mean, I don't want to go on a double date with Mary.

We have even discussed subletting an apartment together. Both of us are getting tired of hotel living. It's okay for a while, but not for a long time. It gets to be a drag. Debbie is straightforward and to the point. You never have to guess what she thinks, but she's got a heart of gold. I'm enclosing a picture of Debbie and me on our weekend we spent in Germany.

I had an interview with J. D. Breaux Decker, a millionaire, and Debbie scheduled a business trip to check up on one of her accounts. We had our business completed by noon on Friday, so we had until Monday morning to see the sights. We stayed in this quaint little bed and breakfast outside the town of Larkspur. Our room had its own fireplace and sitting area. The decor was old-world elegance.

Daddy would die if he could see the big, healthy cows on the hillsides here. The only thing I 'm not crazy about is the German food but I'm just a country girl at heart. Tell Mama I sure wish she could send me a home-cooked meal. The job's even better than I had expected. I even have time for some courses at the university.

Mary's tried to fix me up with several eligible well-to-do bachelors. I politely go out with them at least once to please her. It's a snooze fest, and all they can talk about is themselves. Gag!

She says I need to get out more and have some fun or I'll turn into an old workaholic like her with no one. So far, these dates have been much too focused on themselves and their work to even think I had anything to add to the conversation. The last time Mary came up with Mr. Right, as she called him, he called and said he had a friend traveling with him and did l think I could find him a date? So I railroaded Debbie into going. She had heard all of my reenactments of earlier dates and assured me that this one would be, if nothing else, fun.

We decided to make it easy on them, so we both got ready in my hotel room. Promptly at 8:00 p.m., as scheduled, there was a knock at the door, and there stood the two of them, immaculately dressed young business-men straight out of GQ. I must admit, they were fine looking. We invited them in for a quick drink and some conversation. Debbie decided to set things straight right from the beginning. She said, "Gentlemen, Whitney and I have a strict rule for tonight's date." I couldn't even imagine what was coming next! "None of us may talk about work after we walk out these doors. Tonight is for fun!" You would have thought she had said, "Tonight you must speak only Chinese." I just looked at them and burst out laughing.

It actually turned out to be the best date I'd had in a very long time. We all decided not to do the usual theater and dinner routine, and in-stead we drove into the country to a little out-of-the-way inn. We found out it had been owned and ran by the Robin Stanley family for a hun-dred years. It was not fancy, but it had down-home charm. The staff, all family members, were very pleasant, and the food was wonderful. It was quiet with soft music in the background. Each dining area was a separate little alcove. Ryan and Justin discovered that night that there were other things in life, things unrelated to work. It was good to learn things about

other people that didn't relate to their career. They made us promise to go
out again the next time they had business here.

Ryan and I hit it off and decided to write, but I think he will just be
a buddy—no chemistry! I can't wait to see you! I'd love for you and Deb to
meet also. I have to go for now. Mary and I have actually been invited to
a dinner party honoring Julie Andrews! Can you believe your little sister
is going to eat at the same table as Julie Andrews? I'm still in shock. It's
this Saturday, and Mary has insisted on treating me to my first designer
gown. I continue to be amazed at the famous people Mary knows. Mary
is a hard-core journalist, but she is a journalist with class! She said she
would starve sooner than write some of the trash that's out there today.
This letter comes to you filled with love and hugs!

Love always,
Whitney

Whitney must have written this letter a ways back. At first, I was
confused, especially with her most recent news about her and Mary's in-
terviews and France. Then I noticed the date and it was written over two
weeks ago.

I sure did miss that girl. I was so glad she was seeing the world. Then
I fell asleep, and the next thing I knew, Patsey was knocking at the door.

"Hey, girl. Are you gonna sleep through your wedding?"

"Oh, my goodness, what time is it?"

"It's time you were taking that bubble bath and start getting ready."

I knew I'd chosen my maid of honor well.

Mom, Jessie, and Patsey helped me with my gown. Mom gave me
something old, a locket that had been my grandmother's that she had

been saving for me. Patsey gave me something new, a fancy blue garter. Jessie gave me something borrowed, a pair of antique pearl earrings that Jimmy's dad had given her many years ago. Everything was going as scheduled. There was a knock at the door. It was Daddy. He was standing looking so handsome in his Sunday suit.

"Ladies, if you'll excuse me, I'd like a word with my beautiful daughter, and Jimmy needs a ride to the church. I don't want to give him the chance to skip out."

"Daddy!"

"Just kidding, but I am a little nervous," he said.

Daddy just stood for a few minutes looking at me. He had that happy and sad look on his face. I could tell he was going through all our times together from birth till this day in his mind.

Tears started to well up in his eyes.

"No tears today, my darling. I want this to be the happiest day of your life. I want you to know that no father has ever had a daughter that has given him more joy than you have given me. I'm proud of you, and I know you will be a wonderful wife and mother. Some people need more in their lives to complete them, but you and I are so much alike. All we need to make us complete is the love of our family and the peacefulness of the country."

He came over and gave me a kiss on the forehead and a hug. "Let's get to the church. You've got a good man there nervously waiting to make you, his wife."

The wedding was sweet and simple, and I wouldn't have had it any other way. It was perfect. Mom had set the phone on speaker so that Whitney could be a part of the day.

We had our wedding cake and pictures back at Mom and Dad's. Jimmy told me what he and Dad had been up to all day and I couldn't believe what a great idea it was. We hadn't even thought about what we would do about our wedding night. Well, we knew what we would do, but not where.

We said our goodbyes and headed out to our little cottage in the woods. Jimmy carried me over the threshold, and when he put me down, he looked me in the eyes.

"Well, Mrs. McCoy, any regrets so far?"

"None, Mr. McCoy. I don't suppose you have any thoughts on what we should do now do you?"

"Oh, I believe I could entertain you, possibly in the bedroom."

He lit the fireplace, and I got into my fancy new lingerie. I don't know why we women spend so much on this stuff. We only wear it for a minute or two, but it's a nice touch.

From the moment I joined Jimmy, I lost all sense of time and space. Nothing existed in the world but the two of us. Our first night together as husband and wife was a dream I never wanted to end.

Shortly after daybreak, we were startled by a knock at the door. Jimmy went to see who it could be. Who could be intruding on us? When he opened the door, there stood Daddy.

"I am so sorry to be bothering you two this early, but a Professor Higgins has called three times already. He insisted I come out and get you. He needs Jimmy to call him right away. He said he'd be at his office. I'll go on back and get the coffee on. Come on up when you're ready."

"Jimmy, what could it be?"

"I have no idea, but it must be important. Professor Higgins would not be so persistent."

We showered, and to save time, we got in together, although I'm not sure how much time it actually saved. After we dressed, we headed to Mom and Dad's. Jimmy took the cup of coffee offered to him and went right to the phone. We all sat at the kitchen table, anxiously trying to hear bits and pieces of the conversation.

"I understand. No, I know you had no choice. It's just not exactly what I wanted to hear the day after my wedding day. Yes, I will. Yes, I have all the numbers."

I knew the news was not going to be good. I had already started to dread hearing what the professor had said.

When Jimmy came into the kitchen, he was ashen.

"What is it, Jimmy?" Dawn asked.

"The government will not allow us to go to Bosnia. They aren't letting any more Americans into the country, and they're evacuating the ones that are there as quickly possible."

"Oh, Jimmy, I'm so sorry they've canceled your grant."

"No, not exactly. The location has just been changed. We can still take advantage of the money that has already been set aside for this project, but we will have to leave first thing in the morning."

Jimmy came over and knelt down in front of me. "Dawn, for the first time in my life, I was almost hoping that the project had been canceled. I'm so sorry."

I stroked his hair. "Jimmy, this is a lifetime dream of yours, and I was so worried about you going to Bosnia to begin with. Where are you going?"

"Mozambique. They are really in need of our help, and this is our only chance at salvaging the project. I don't know how I will be able to leave you."

"I know. I feel the exact same way, but we knew this time was coming soon. The sooner you leave, the sooner you'll be home to me. Just remember you're a married man!"

"Dawn, that's something you'll never have to worry about."

"You have to go today, don't you?"

"Yes."

"Oh, Jimmy, I promised myself I wouldn't cry." It was too late. I had totally forgotten about everyone else. They had gone back into the living room when Jimmy came to me with the news. "Okay, enough of that. Let's get you ready to go, and I promise I'll try my best not to make this any harder than it is."

"Dawn, we haven't even talked about what you're going to do. Are you going back to school right away, or are you staying on here for a while?"

"I'm not sure myself yet, but everything will be fine. I do not want you to worry about me. You go and show all those people what a smart and talented husband I have."

It was a tearful farewell when Jimmy and Jessie drove away. Jessie had needed to get back to her farm and it was on Jimmy's way, so she decided she'd ride along with her son. I stood and watched until the car carrying my new husband was a mere speck. Then Jimmy was gone, and I felt more alone than I had ever felt in my life.

Daddy came over to comfort me, and I told him I wanted to go back to the cottage and spend some time alone.

"You take all the time you need, and I won't let your mom hover. You've got your car, so whenever you're ready, come on up. If you decide to move into the cottage, we'll need to get you a phone hooked up."

"I love you, Daddy, but I have a cell phone. Don't worry about me."

CHAPTER 23

A rush or emotions hit me when I walked into the house. I felt drained, so I lay down on the bed that my husband and I had shared not so many hours ago. I pulled his pillow to my face, and I could smell his scent. I closed my eyes and relived our night together and drifted into a deep sleep. When I awoke, daylight was beginning to fade away. I slept the entire day away.

I wondered where Jimmy was right now and what he was doing.

There hadn't been time to get the particulars of the trip.

I went into the bathroom to wash the sleep from my eyes, and taped to the mirror was an envelope.

To my darling wife.

My eyes filled with tears at once as I began to read.

I know right about now you're feeling alone and sad and somewhat abandoned. Please don't! You have no idea how hard this is for me to do. My entire career has been working toward this opportunity. I never imagined that I would meet my true love along the way. I knew from the first time I saw you in the diner that you were the woman who would complete my life. I want you to know that I consider myself the luckiest man in the world. The only way I could make the decision to fulfill this dream of mine, is because in my heart I know that you understand me completely. For the pain you are feeling, I am so very sorry. I would never intentionally cause you to be unhappy. You never really told me in so many words what you wanted to do while I'm away, but I have a feeling college and a career is not what you want. You make whatever decision is necessary to make you happy and our life together more fulfilling. I trust you completely in all that you do, and I want you to know that you will be in my thoughts and in my heart every day that I live.

You have such unconditional love, and I can't wait for us to have children and live our lives together as husband and wife until the end of time. I feel so blessed with love and opportunity that I have this deep need to teach and help others to have a better quality of life.

So, my darling, this is a thank-you from the bottom of my heart for understanding my need to complete this project. Mom told me that she has never been happier in her life because now she not only has a son but two daughters that she loves dearly. She made me promise to tell you that she's always there for you if you ever need her. I don't want you to worry about money. We are by no means rich, but in the dresser are the checkbook and the savings book in both our names. There will also be a direct deposit monthly. The paperwork for that is there also. I haven't had anything to spend my money on for years, so use it as you see fit. Make a home for us wherever you choose. I'm not sure how long it will be before I can contact you directly. Just as soon as I can, I will be in touch. I do know the flight will take around eighteen hours. You are my love, my life, and my happiness. I'll be counting the days until I see your beautiful face again and can hold you in my arms.

All my love,
Jimmy

By the end of the letter, the tears had been replaced with a sense of happiness and contentment. This man that I had known for such a short time seemed to have a window to my soul. He knew my thoughts and desires without me speaking. I was not going to be weepy and sad anymore. I had so much to do this year I just wouldn't have time to feel sorry for myself. If I did, I'd just reread this letter.

The next morning was one of the most beautiful that I'd experienced. It had rained during the night, and across the sky was a magnificent rainbow. As I sat on the front porch with my mug of coffee, the animals came from the woods surrounding the cottage, seeming to be coming up and introducing themselves. A family of squirrels was scampering around in the leaves; one of the little ones even came right up on the railing and sat looking at me. I decided to get a squirrel feeder and put it in a corner of the porch so it would come visit again. The others were more reluctant to come up close. They would run up one at a time as if to warn the little one of possible danger and then run back and watch from a distance. I felt compelled to give this little guy a name. Happy—I know he's not a dwarf, but he just looks happy. Even though there weren't seven of them, I could definitely see a Grouchy, a Bashful, and a Dopey.

There was a noise at the edge of the woods that finally scared Happy from his place on the rail. I wish I had my camera loaded and ready because there was a mother deer and her baby cautiously walking into the clearing. The mother deer stopped and looked around, ever protective of her baby. The baby scampered around on its wobbly legs, playing in the tall grass chasing a butterfly. All the while, the mother stood in a protective stance.

Oh, how I longed for a baby of my own to love and nurture, a little person made from both Jimmy and me. Children would just make our circle of life complete. I knew Jimmy would be a good and loving father. The letter he had written me had been just what I needed. It had changed the sad, sorrowful feeling into one of happy anticipation of our life together. I was exhilarated this morning, ready to get going with my new life as wife and homemaker, the life I had always dreamed of. The sky was a little bluer, and the smells around me a little sweeter on this brand-new day. Just then, I noticed the mother deer and her baby dash back into the woods. Sure enough, there was a reason: Daddy's truck was coming down the lane.

"Good morning!"

"Hi, Daddy, anything wrong?"

"No, I just had a message for you from Professor Higgins."

"Professor Higgins? Are you sure nothing's wrong?"

"Yep, he just wanted me to assure you that he would let you know of any news as soon as he hears from the group. He said they were to call from...some town. I'm sorry I can't remember the name, but apparently it will be the town closest to where Jimmy will be setting up his headquarters, and it has a phone. He said it's a forty-five minute drive from the town to the site for the headquarters. I guess Jimmy will be calling him before they start their journey to their final destination. He also wanted me to pass on an apology for the untimely change in plans and to let you know to call him if there is anything you need or if you have any concerns along the way, He seems like a pretty good guy. He said he had a family member on this trip too. So, how'd you sleep?"

"I slept great. I just love it out here. I've been sitting here watching the animals. I didn't know Professor Higgins had family on the trip. Did he have any idea of when Jimmy might be calling?"

"No, he said he didn't know."

"Have you decided what you're gonna do yet?"

"I'm pretty sure I'll be dropping out of school and coming back to the cottage, but if you would hold off on telling Mom, I would appreciate it. I'm not 100 percent sure yet."

"Okay, I'll promise to hold off on telling her if you'll promise me that whatever decision you make will be the one that makes you happy, not Mom or me."

"Either way, I need to go back for my things and to take care of details, bills, and what not. I don't want Patsey to feel abandoned." Dawn sighed.

"When is Donna coming home?" Bob asked.

"Not for about 1 and a half weeks. You know, I should probably call Jessie and let her know what Professor Higgins had to say."

"Yes, I'm sure she's just as anxious for information about Jimmy as you are. You know, I haven't talked to you about this yet, but I knew Jimmy's dad. He was a good man, and anyone who knew him felt he had been set up. That Frank MacIntosh really ruined Sam and Jessie's life together. No one had the right to affect another person's life like that. I never trusted that man, but your mom and I tried to overlook it because we loved Donna. Shoot, at times it was like she was one of our daughters."

"This year has been full of surprises. It's made me take a fresh look at life. I hope you know how thankful I am for the kind of home life you and Mom gave Whitney and me. We had all we ever needed. We had love."

"I'd better be gettin' back to my work. Give me a holler when you decide what you're gonna do." Bob said.

As Daddy was pulling away, he leaned out the window and yelled, "You should take Queenie for a ride. It'll do you both good."

CHAPTER 24

Later that day as I rode my horse, I realized how much I'd missed riding. Queenie and I were right in sync as usual. I had loved this horse ever since the first time I'd laid eyes on her at the fairgrounds. Otis Tucker, who breeds some of the finest horses in the territory, had her there to sell. I guess I hung around the stalls so much he figured he'd just put me to work. I asked him so many questions about that one special horse that it was obvious I wanted it. I was only ten, but I had no problem keeping up with the other workers there to keep the stables clean and the horses fed and exercised. As a matter of fact, Mr. Tucker told me I was his best worker.

"Girlie, why don't you just ask your pa to buy you this horse?"

"Daddy already told me I can't have a horse until I can earn the money to buy one and know about takin' care of it. He says it would be all my responsibility."

"Well, I can tell that you know how to take care of a horse. Have you saved any money?"

"Oh, yes, sir. I have saved $178.95, but I'm sure that horse is much more than that."

"You're right there. She's one of my best. I plumb forgot, I owe you for helping' me out after school and on Saturdays. I'd be happy to hire you. Then you could get that horse sooner."

I was happy Mr. Tucker wanted to hire me, but I didn't want just any horse. I wanted that one. I'd even named her Queenie after my grandpa's favorite horse.

I guess Mr. Tucker could see the love between Queenie and me because the next day he told me if Queenie didn't sell by the next week, he'd make me a deal where I could pay her off. I'd have to leave her with him until it was paid, but I didn't care. He also said Mom and Dad would have to approve the whole deal first. That day when I left, I ran home. Daddy was out plowing the north field, and I couldn't wait for him to come back in, so I ran out to meet him.

I was so out of breath when I reached him that he thought Something was wrong at the house. He jumped down right away.

"What's wrong?"

"Nothing. I was just too excited to wait for you to get home."

After I told him what Mr. Tucker had offered, he, as usual, said that he and Mom had to talk it over first. When he saw my disappointment, he added, "I'll put in a good word for you with Mom."

He must have because Mom agreed I could give it a try. Mom did have a good question.

"What will you do if Queenie sells this week? I don't want you to agree to work for Mr. Tucker and then be so disappointed you can't continue if he is counting on your help."

"I wouldn't do that, Mom. I'll work for him even if Queenie gets sold to someone else. I'm not a baby anymore. I know there's a chance I won't end up with her."

Well, Queenie, I am certainly glad that at ten I was so persistent.

As I rode back, I watched the sun set over the pond. It melted so slowly, it was as though it didn't want to give up the day.

Mom and Daddy will be getting ready for supper soon. It would please Mom if I popped in and ate with them. After all, I had to brush Queenie down and get her put up for the night. Maybe if I stayed out here, Daddy could fix it so that I could keep Queenie at the cottage. There was already fencing all around and good pasture land.

Daddy's truck was gone, and there was a minivan in the driveway. I hurried as I put Queenie up. I wanted to go into the house to see if Daddy had gone to the cottage with word from Jimmy. I would definitely need to take my phone wherever I go from now on. As I neared the kitchen door, I could hear women's voices. One sounded rather familiar, but I couldn't tell who it was.

"Oh, Dawn, honey, have you come for supper?"

"I thought I would if you have enough."

"You know I never got used to cookin for two. Of course I do. You remember Beth Cornwell, don't you?"

"Sure, how've you been?" I asked, although it was plain to see she was heartbroken about something. "Are Janet and Allison still living around here?"

"No, honey, they've both moved away. I just heard that you just got married. I am so happy for you. Listen, Ida, I have to be running and you need to finish your cookin'. Dawn, it was great to see you again."

"Thank you, you too." Then I overheard her thank Mom for listening and being such a good friend.

"That poor woman," Mom said after she'd left.my heart goes out to her. Sometimes I lose sight of how lucky I am. You and Whitney have never caused your dad and me any problems."

"What's wrong? Are Janet and Allison in some kind of trouble?" Dawn asked, with a worried look on her face.

"Janet was missing for six months, and when Beth finally heard from her, she was in pretty bad shape. She is involved in drugs and alcohol and basically living on the streets in a pretty bad area. Allison just went up and left town about a month ago without telling Beth, and she owes her mom five thousand dollars. Beth took out a loan and then gave her the money with the understanding that she was to make the payments on the loan. Allison convinced her she was gonna get her life together with the kids. Instead, she

handed the kids over to her ex-husband and left Beth to pay the money back herself.

Beth and Dave are both working at the hardware store that

they bought about three years ago, and between working together and all the problems with the girls, it's put a strain on their marriage."

"No wonder she sounded so down. I almost didn't recognize her. She looks ten years older than the last time I saw her."

"Well, stress can do that to a person. I just wish those girls would realize that they're slowly killing their mother. You know, no matter how old your kids get or what they do, you love them and worry about them." Mom said.

"I never knew you and Mrs. Cornwell were good friends."

"Beth and I were as close as you and Donna when we were in school together, and even though we haven't seen much of each other over the years, we have kept in touch. She quit school and married Bruce Brown, who turned out to be an alcoholic who ran from one woman to the other throughout their whole marriage. I always suspected that he was physically abusive to her.

Then she married David Cornwell, and it looked as though she would finally have the happiness she deserved. But Janet and Allison have taken turns breaking her heart over and over again. I'm afraid she is gonna have a nervous breakdown. She has always tried to do as good as she could for her children, but I think she's finally lost hope. In high school, she was popular and so smart. She was in the honor society and head majorette. She just made some bad choices, and they've ruined her life," Mom was teary eyed when she talked about her friend.

"I should have been there for her, even if she shied away from everyone."

"I know, but when your children turn on you—well, that's more than a mother can take."

"Mom, I feel sorry for Mrs. Cornwell, but you can't change a person unless they want to change." "If I were you, I'd just let her know how much you value her friendship. Maybe invite her to church, Pastor Michaels has been known to inspire quite a few people."

———//———

CHAPTER 25

A couple of days after my encounter with Beth Cornwell in Mom's kitchen, I was on my way to OJC. I couldn't help but think about how much pain this woman had to deal with. Janet and Allison were both older than me, so I really didn't know them well. I do remember babysitting for Allison's children a couple of times. She was always very nice to me, but she was always quite a partier.

Every time I went over to babysit, I felt like I had to clean.

The house was always a disaster and the kids needed to be bathed.

There were never any clean clothes in their drawers, and

what had been washed was in stacks all over the living room. I must say, though, the kids seemed happy, and none of them ever talked badly about their mother.

It did worry me at times when I left because, Allison and her husband were usually pretty drunk when they came home. I always prayed that the kids would stay asleep and that they'd be safe. It's strange how some kids who have hardly any mothering manage to survive.

I can't imagine hurting my parents like that after all they had done for me. According to Mom, Beth Cornwell had always been a loving mother. She did everything she could for her children, maybe too much.

Before I knew it, I was turning into our driveway. I was almost glad that Patsey was at work. I didn't really feel like talking tonight. I missed being in the little cottage. For some reason, when I was there, I felt closer to Jimmy. Morning would be here much too quickly. I really dreaded going back to school. I had to decide soon.

Maybe I would give Whitney a call. I wanted to hear her voice and talk things over with her.

When the answering machine came on, my heart sank a little.

This was ridiculous! I'd write to her. It always helped me to write my thoughts down. More times than not, it cleared my mind. After writing letters to both Whitney and Jimmy, I was feeling a little queasy, so I decided to go down for a ginger ale.

"Hey, girl, when did you get home?"

"Hi. Oh, a couple of hours ago. I thought you had to work tonight."

"I was supposed to, but we were so slow that Doug told me I could leave early. Any news from Jimmy?" asked Patsey

"No, not yet. I'm not even sure how long it will be until I do hear from him. Professor Higgins called and said he would let me know any news as soon as he hears from them. His granddaughter is on the trip too. She's a nurse. "Dawn replied.

"I was reading about the project in the paper this morning. I saved it for you. There's a picture of the whole team and a little bit about each of them. They make that cousin of mine sound pretty important." Just then Patsey looked at her strangely. "Are you feeling, okay?"

"I think I may be getting the flu. I don't know. Maybe I'm just tired."

"I'm gonna go get some take-out food and a movie. Can I bring you something?"

"No, thanks, I don't feel like eating anything."Patsey hadn't been gone long, and I was looking over the

article. There he was—my Jimmy. I wished he were here with me right now.

Then I noticed Professor Higgons' granddaughter, Kelly Higgons, wow, she's drop dead gorgeous.

I thought, Kelly Higgins, you had better stay away from my man because you are much too pretty.

I got up to get some more soda, and I felt as though I would pass out. What was wrong with me? I hoped Patsey would get home soon. Something was wrong. I'd never felt like this before.

"Hey, I'm home with food and flicks. Dawn, what's wrong? You look as white as a sheet."

"Let me get you a cold cloth. You lay down here on the couch and put your feet up. Did you eat today?"

I never answered any of Patsey's questions, but she didn't seem to notice.

"Patsey, I think you're gonna have to help me get to the bathroom. I'm going to be sick."

Okay, then I'm taking you to the emergency room, and I don't want any arguments." Patsey said sternly.

"I'm too sick to argue anyway."

Patsey had me at the hospital in record time. She let me out at the entrance to the emergency room and went on to park the car. I was thankful that it seemed to be a slow night for emergencies. The nurse at the desk got all the information she needed from me and hustled me off to a little cubicle where she left me to wait for the doctor on call. Another nurse came in for all of the vitals, blood pressure, and whatnot. She had me put on one of those lovely paper gowns and assured me it wouldn't be long before the doctor would be in.

In about five minutes, an extremely good-looking man, probably in his late twenties, appeared in the doorway.

"Hello, I'm Dr. Beaumont, Matt Beaumont. I see by your files you've been dizzy, nauseated, and more tired than usual. Mrs. McCoy, is it possible you could be pregnant?"

The thought had not crossed my mind. Pregnant! Of course it was possible. Jimmy and I hadn't always been too careful, especially when we had been in Jamaica. That night on the beach had been totally spontaneous. Matt Beaumont just stood as I sat speechless, looking at me and waiting for a response to his question.

"I suppose anything is possible," I finally blurted out.

"Well, there's no reason to worry about it yet. We'll run some tests, and then we'll know for sure."

My word, now he thinks I don't want to be pregnant. I wouldn't be upset if I found out I'm pregnant. It just never crossed my mind. I was thinking more on the lines of the flu. Actually, I'd be quite happy.

"Is your husband with you? No, he's out of the country on business. He is a professor at the college, and he left not long ago for Mozambique."

"Do you mean Jimmy McCoy."

"Yes, Jimmy's my husband."

"He and I are old friends. As a matter of fact, I just recently met his cousin, Patsey, at the diner. She's quite a woman, but she won't give me the time of day. She's always too busy."

"That's Patsey all right."

"Okay, I'll get the nurse and we'll see if we can't figure out what's going on to make you feel so bad."

As Patsey waited in the waiting room, she caught a glimpse of Matt Beaumont as he went in and out of the cubicles. She was glad he didn't notice her. It had been hard enough sidestepping his flirtations at the diner, but now as she looked at him, she wondered what it would be like to be in his arms, to touch his lips to hers until their bodies merely melted together. He had eyes that seemed to mesmerize you and a smile that made you feel good all over. But, damn it, she had no time for romance, she had a job and a degree to earn. She was going to make something of herself.

He was a doctor, after all. How could he be interested in someone like her? He had probably just been playing around, flirting with her when he came in for his dinner, which he did at least four or five times a week. She was sure, there was some ninety-pound nurse or model just waiting around for the good doctor.

Pretty soon, Dawn was coming out, and she already looked much better. She even had a smile on her face.

"Well, it looks as though you've made a miraculous recovery."

"Oh, I should be all better in about six months."

Patsey forgot she was in a hospital and let out a squeal that had the receptionist looking right at us. "You don't mean it. You're pregnant?"

"I certainly am."

"I don't know why neither of us thought of that."

"Me either, but isn't it wonderful?" They stood there in the waiting room, hugging and giggling.

Matt walked up behind them with a bag in his hand. "You forgot your prenatal package, Dawn."

"Oh, thank you, Dr. Beaumont."

"Hello, Patsey. Not working tonight?"

"No, even the wicked get some time off." As she said it, she remembered he had asked her about a late movie and she had told him she had to work late. She thought, Oh well, he couldn't have been serious anyway, or could he? He did have a strange look in his eyes. He looked both mad and hurt. Thank God Dawn was there.

"I just told Patsey the good news," Dawn said. "Patsey, Matt tells me he and Jimmy are friends."

Patsey just smiled a somewhat chilling smile as Dr. Matt Beaumont leered at her.

Dawn thought, there's definitely something there, whether either of them know it or not, that's the question.

Patsey said, "Hey, girl, we'd better get you home for some rest. After all, you've got a baby to think of now."

"I suppose you're right. Thank you again, doctor, for all your help and for the good news."

Matt seemed to have softened up again and was most gracious. "I really only reported the news. I had nothing to do with it." He no sooner said it than he wished he'd picked his words more wisely. He turned three shades of red.

Patsey looked back at him and said, "I didn't know doctors got embarrassed." She chuckled as the door closed behind her and Dawn.

In the car, she was rattling on about the baby and Jimmy and baby showers and on and on.

"Hold on, woman!" Dawn said.

"I know I'm getting carried away, but I'm so happy for you and Jimmy."

"Patsey, I have a favor to ask of you, and I hope you'll understand."

Patsey looked a bit puzzled but just sat waiting for Dawn to go on.

"I'm not going to tell Jimmy that I'm pregnant, at least not right now."

"Why not? He'll be on cloud nine."

"I know, but I don't want anything to interfere with his work. I don't want him to feel any more guilty than he already does for being so far away. He has waited for this opportunity for a long time, and I want him to be able to complete his dream without worrying about me and the baby."

"I'm not sure I agree, but I'll keep my mouth shut as long as there are no complications. You know you'll have to take Aunt Jessie into your confidence."

"I know. There's one more thing, I've decided to move back to the little cottage behind my parents' house and drop out of school. I never wanted a career. I enrolled more for my mom's sake than for me. This is all I ever wanted, to be married and raise a family. I just feel more comfortable in the country, and I love the cottage."

"Honey, you need to be wherever you are the happiest. I will miss you, but it's not like you're so far away that I can't come visit. How do you think your mom will take the news?"

"Well, I do have the advantage of first telling her she's gonna be a grandmother, so that should soften the blow some she's always known that my heart is in the country and that I'm just a simple person with simple needs like Daddy. She'll have to be satisfied with one daughter being a professional. Dr. Beaumont even recommended an OB in Bradleyville. His Sister Julie has just set up her practice there. By the way, what's up with you and the good doctor?"

Patsey, looking a little flushed, said, "Whatever do you mean?"

"Come on, give. I could tell there was something between the two of you."

"Oh, it's nothing. He comes in Maple Street for dinner a few times a week and he asked me out a few times."

"And why haven't you gone out with him? He's very good-looking, and he's obviously interested in you."

"I don't have timefor dating. I have work and studying. That pretty much takes up my time."

"You know if you don't take out some time for yourself, you could burn out."

"Well, to be perfectly honest, I have been thinking about weakening. He is rather hot. He may not ask me again, though. He asked me out for tonight, but I told him I had to work late. I didn't know we would end up at the hospital and he would catch me in a lie."

"So, call him."

"We'll see. Enough about me—how are you feeling?"

"Pretty good, actually. Matt gave me something to settle my stomach, and the news kind of overshadows the nausea."

When we got home, there were three messages on the machine. One was from Donna letting us know she got home and to call her as soon as we get in, and one was from Professor Higgins: "I heard from Jimmy. They have arrived safely and are continuing on to set up camp.

He made me promise to call you no matter how late and to tell you that he would be in touch soon. I do apologize for calling so late."

The third one was for Patsey from Matthew Beaumont: "Patsey, since you said you had to work late and you didn't, you owe me. Call and tell me about your next evening off because we have a date. If I don't hear from you, I will know that you are just not interested in me, and I promise to leave you alone. I'm hoping that you'll call."

"Thank God. I can breathe a little easier just knowing Jimmy got there safely. Do you think we should call Donna this late?"

"Sure, we have big news for her, and I'm dying to hear from her."

"Hey, don't you have a call to make yourself?"

"Okay, I'll call, then let's call Donna."

I gave Patsey some privacy, and when she had hung up, she came into the kitchen with a big grin on her face. "You'll be happy to know that Dr. Matt and I have a date for this weekend."

Donna picked the phone up on the first ring. "Where have you two been so late?"

"Are you sitting down?" Dawn asked.

"What's wrong? Has something happened?" Donna inquired.

"Settle down, everything is fine. It's just that our kids will probably be going to school together, that's all."

"Our kids? You're pregnant! Frank, Dawn is pregnant! Oh, I wish I was there to hug you right now. Frank says Congratulations. Are you feeling, okay? When is your due date? I have so many questions." "They will have to wait because Patsey and I Have questions,

we want to hear about the honeymoon first."

"Oh, it was spectacular. We had the best time, but we're both glad to be home so we can really start our life together in our own home with our friends and families. Speaking of families, I just talked to Mom, and she didn't mention anything about you being pregnant."

"She doesn't know yet. I just found out myself." I explained the situation about Jimmy and not putting more guilt on him than he has by telling him. I wanted to tell Jessie and my parents in person. I also told her about my plans, and she was pleased to know that I was coming home so, we could see each other more often.

"Here, let me put Patsey on."

"Hey, girl, how's married life? I know, isn't it great? Listen, you probably will want to rent this place out and make some money on it for a change. I can find a smaller place." Patsey said.

"Patsey, I do not want to rent our house to strangers. Why don't you find a roommate? That is, if you want to. I know it will probably be lonely in that big house alone. You do whatever you think is best for you. What's this I hear about a doctor?"

"Don't even get me started. I'll let you know after we've had our first date. I'll put Dawn back on."

"You guys can come visit me from time to time, you know." Donna said pleadingly.

It was good to hear Donna's voice. She was so happy now. She had a real family at last!

—//—

CHAPTER 26

The next few months went by fairly quickly. As much as Patsey protested, she and Matt were an item. He promised not to crowd her and to give her time for her studies. She said he comes over and fixes dinner while she studies, and he reads his medical journals while she does her work. She even cut back on her hours at the diner.

Dad came and helped me move one day when Mom and Beth Cornwall were at a craft fair in North Carolina. After hearing my news, she didn't seem to mind at all that I had dropped school. She started knitting blankets and booties, and Dad was busy making a cradle. All in all, they were happy grandparents-to-be. Jessie agreed not to tell Jimmy as long as there were no complications. She and Mom had been spending more and more time together, which was great. Shortly after I got moved in, Jimmy's first letter tracked me down. I had my first visit with Julie Beaumont, and she was just as nice as her brother. They looked a lot alike—dark hair, big brown eyes, and she was always smiling. She told me I might go through some mood swings. Boy, was she right. I found myself either extremely happy or crying over the silliest things. In a way, Jimmy was probably lucky he didn't have to go through it.

Jimmy's letters were so descriptive. I could tell he had already become good friends with another member of the group, Duffy, He was kind of a jack-of-all-trades. He was a medic as well as a mechanic, and, according to Jimmy, he could make anything they needed out of whatever was at hand. I could almost hear the laughter in his voice when he told stories about Duffy. It seemed he was quite the character. He managed to make some wine out of the local berries, and I guess one night he drank so much that on the way to their makeshift outhouse, he slipped and fell into the feeble structure. It fell down around him. He just stood there totally in the open, unzipped his pants, and went about his business. The next day when Jimmy asked him how he was feeling, he replied, "Never better, but what the hell happened to the outhouse?" Jimmy told him what had happened, and he just roared with laughter. He said, "Guess I'll have to build the next one a bit stronger."

Professor Higgins's granddaughter, Keleigh, is the resident nurse both for the group and for the locals. She is giving the local children exams and catching them up on shots. She is very good with people and very useful in that she speaks about six foreign languages. Her fiancé is in the marines and is also out of the country for a while. I'm not sure where he's located, but she said she's grateful to be busy, so she doesn't feel so lonely. I told her I know all about feeling lonely. I have shown everyone your picture, and they all agree that I must be the luckiest man in the world to have such a beautiful and understanding wife. I, of course, agree!

The camp itself is very modest and mostly made up of large tents for the quarters, a lean-to and tent for the kitchen, a dining area, makeshift stalls for showering, and, of course, the outhouse. Duffy is in charge of building a more permanent structure to be used for the kitchen and dining hall that we will leave for the local residents to hopefully use for a school after we leave. Duffy has worked out quite a barter system. In exchange for helping with the building process, he helps them to renovate their homes. All in all, it has worked out quite well.

We planned with one of the local women to do the laundry for the entire group. In exchange, we have chosen their property to do our first experimental garden. We will all benefit from the first harvest, and by the time we are ready to leave, she and her husband and children can also reap the rewards from it for a long time to come. There is a mission church that is the only source of education in this area. It is also the only hope for any children who have either been abandoned or left orphaned. They have very limited funds and only five nuns to do the work and teaching. We went over this past Sunday and organized a baseball game for the kids. Dawn, it was heartwarming to see the smiles on those little faces. Most of them knew nothing about the game, but they picked it up quickly. We decided to make the mission our second garden project. They can use all the help they can get. It's a good thing you aren't here because I know you would want to bring a car load of these kids home to mother. There are four little babies that were literally left on the doorstep, so this is the only family they will know. Paul and Doris, the only married couple in our group, are teachers by profession, so they are going to contact the powers that be in the States and try to get some school supplies and textbooks sent over. They are training three very eager young people to be teachers. They will be able to help the nuns and lighten their load a little bit. Most of the people are so grateful for any help we can give them. Of course, there are those who regard us as intruders and want no part of the program, but for the most part, I am pleased and feel like we can make a difference.

Well, babe, I have to get some sleep. Morning comes all too early around here. Please send more pictures and write all about What's going on with you? I read your letters over and over. I miss you always, but the nights are the worst.

Until we are together again, I remain your loving husband,
Jimmy

Donna was so excited that I had decided to move back home. She said if we only had Whitney back, it would be like old times.

We got together every day and talked about babies and such. We call Patsey at least twice a week. She found a roommate, Lisa Murphy. Patsey said she met her at the diner, and they became friends. She's different than anyone I've ever known, but I can tell she's a good person. She's from New York City, so she's a little posh. She'd been staying with friends of her parents and really wanted to find a place of her own.

Patsey said, "I gave her Donna's room, and she absolutely loves the house. I'm hoping you can come to visit me soon because I want you to meet her and let me know that you approve of my choice. I know it's not necessary, but I still want you all to meet."

Donna switched doctors because I was crazy about Dr. Beaumont. Of course, Donna, being the eternal matchmaker, is hell-bent on finding Julie a love interest. Since Julie's new in town, the three of us became pretty good friends.

All in all, life was good. I was so happy to be carrying Jimmy's baby and to be home with family and friends. When I read Jimmy's letters, Donna switched doctors because I was crazy about Dr. Beaumont. Of course, Donna, being the eternal matchmaker, is hell-bent on finding

Julie a love interest. Since Julie's new in town, the three of us became pretty good friends.

I could tell he was happy. His work was going even better than he had

hoped. It was one of those times when you felt like it was too good to be

true, like just around the corner something bad was bound

to happen.

CHAPTER 27

Meanwhile, across the miles, it was very early in the morning when Preston, Mary's lawyer and longtime friend, came knocking at Whitney's door.

Dazed and still groggy from sleep, Whitney staggered to the door. Debbie was right on her heels.

"Who in the world is at our door at this hour?"

"I don't know, but someone this early can't be bringing good news." When Whitney opened the door, there stood Preston, his face drawn and pale. From his looks, Debbie had been right. It certainly didn't appear to be good. Preston, who had always been one of the most articulate people Whitney had ever known, now stood murmuring under his breath, and Whitney couldn't understand a thing he was saying. She did pick up something about Mary.

"Preston, please come in and sit down. Can I get you some coffee?"

He just sat there, limp. Debbie went to fix them some coffee, and Whitney asked, "You mentioned Mary. Is she okay?"

"No, she will never be okay again!"

"What do you mean? What is wrong?"

Now he sat, worried beyond reason. Whitney became impatient.

"Preston, please speak up and go slowly so I can understand you."

Preston reached over and took Whitney's hands in his. Gently stroking them, he began.

"Mary has been murdered. She was murdered right in her own home in her bed, "he had apparently been holding his emotions for as long as he could because at this point, he broke down and wept.

"Oh my god, I was just with her last night. How could something like this happen? How did you find out?"

"Mamie, her housekeeper, found her when she went in as she did every morning. She found Mary slumped over in her bed, her evening teacup spilled all over the spread and broken on the floor. So far, the police believe she was poisoned."

"Wouldn't Mamie have known if someone else was in the house?"

"She is blaming herself for that very thing right now. The police said that the murderer didn't have to have been there last night. They could have known Mary's schedule and habits and planted the poison days ago. They aren't sure exactly where the poison was put, but they think it was in either the tea or the sugar."

"My god, that means they could have killed Mamie, too, or anyone, for that matter."

Debbie asked, "Did Mary serve you tea last night when you were there?"

"No, Mary knew I wasn't a tea drinker, and I was in kind of a hurry. I told her you and I had dinner plans, and then we were off to the theater. I feel so bad because I think she may have wanted to talk, and I just rushed out with the additions to the book she needed me to proof and retype." Whitney started to cry, out of guilt, and loss. She had loved Mary, both as a friend and a mentor.

"Honey, you didn't know." Preston said comfortingly.

Debbie brought in our coffee, and Preston took it in shaky hands.

At the site of Whitney crying, Debbie asked "Whit, are you okay? I know how very close you and Mary were. This has got to be a tremendous shock."

"I just can't believe it, you know? It doesn't seem possible that I'll not see her pecking away at her computer, or her going over research materials."

Preston began to speak again, a little more composed. "Mary has been working on a piece that would expose a major drug smuggling ring. They worked out of London and New York. I don't know all the details, but I know she only trusted one other person completely, Detective Snyder. I also know they were closing in. I guess they got a little too close. Mary knew she was in danger. She had even been threatened. I begged her to just let the police handle it and forget it, but you know how stubborn she was when she latched onto a story, especially this one. She said it was personal.

"Mary was in my office yesterday afternoon and left an envelope for me to give you in the event that anything happened to her. I hope you know how very much she thought of you. She told me that you were like the daughter she had never allowed herself to have. She was always too busy traveling from one foreign country to another. I myself proposed to her some twenty years ago, but she told me we were much too close to ruin it by marrying. She said, she loved me too much to make me live with a compulsive workaholic." Preston seemed to drift for a while into his memories, so I sat patiently until he was ready to resume.

"Please forgive me, but I do miss her so. Anyway, on to business. Mary Whitman has left everything she owns to you, my dear." Whitney replied, in total shock,

"She already gave me too much. Doesn't she have family?"

"The only family left is a nephew, and she was quite insistent that he get nothing. I believe he was involved in the drug smuggling, maybe even her murderer!"

"Why would her own nephew want to kill her?" Whitney asked.

"Five years ago, her sister, Constance, died. She had been ill for a long time, and Mary kept her here with a private nurse for her last year. All she wanted was to see her son again before she died. Trying to grant her sister's dying wish, she hired a private detective to try to find him. They came close many times, but he always managed to elude them. Mary and Constance's parents were Elizabeth and Thomas Whitman. The Whitman family had been in English high society for hundreds of years. They even hobnobbed with the royal family. Thomas was the last of the line, and since he had only daughters, it would end with him. While on a trip to Paris, Constance met and married Phillip Fontaine. He recognized the Whitman name at once when introduced to Constance and pursued her with a vengeance. Not being much of a beauty, she was totally taken in by his attention.

"Even though her parents were devastated that she had married a virtual stranger, they tried to accept Philip into the family for her sake. It didn't take long for Fontaine to show his true colors. He began to go through Constance's money in no time flat. Not being a fool, Thomas Whitman had him checked out and found that this was not the first wealthy woman that he had married and left as soon as the money ran out. By the time Constance realized why he had married her, she was pregnant, and for fear of what he might do to the baby, she had spoken to the police, a detective Bud Snyder. She told him that Phillip had been physically abusive. She told Snyder that she was telling Phillip that she was leaving him, so Snyder said he would be in the other room for protection. When Constance told him he had to get out, he pulled a knife on her. Officer Snyder heard the noise and busted in just in time to knock Fontaine off-balance. He quickly righted himself and, full of rage, lunged forward with full intent on killing Snyder. All Constance saw was blood, and detective Snyder fell to the ground. So filled with fear for herself and her unborn child, she grabbed the gun that Phillip kept in the desk drawer and shot him. She kept firing until he finally fell motionless to the ground.

"Snyder started to revive enough to call for help.

Constance was never the same again.

She moved back in with her parents. The baby was born two months later. It was a son, Joshua Whitman. She took back her family name, not wanting any association with Phillip Fontaine.

"The child wanted for nothing. Between the grandparents and the guilt-ridden mother, they virtually spoiled him rotten. It seems that the apple didn't fall far from the tree where he was concerned. He got into trouble from the first year of high school, and of course his mother got him out. He was thrown out of three different universities. Thomas finally cut his money off, and he disappeared. His family never saw him again.

"Thomas and Elizabeth both died in a car crash a month after his disappearance. Constance took to drinking and taking sedatives and couldn't be trusted alone. She'd had a weak heart from childhood, and this worsened her condition. Mary finally had to move her in with her under the care of a full-time nurse until her death. I'm kind of jumping around, I know, but it's a mixed-up story. Anyway, back to the detective that Mary had hired to try to find Joshua, who was going by Phillip Fontaine now. He was carrying on his father's profession as a con artist. He was conning elderly rich women into investing their money in companies that didn't exist and taking off with their life savings. Wanting to end his life of crime, Mary and Detective Bud Snyder led the police right to him and handed over the evidence needed to put him away.

"Mary asked to speak to him after he was sentenced. She asked him why he didn't even bother to come to his mother's funeral and all he said was, 'The bitch killed my father. It served her right.' The detective who worked with Mary back then was Bud Snyder, the detective that had saved her sister's life. He is the same one working on this drug scam."

"Shouldn't you call him? He could be the next victim." inquired Whitney.

"I already did. He's flying in tonight. He had some interesting news. It seems Joshua was released six months ago. If it's okay with you, I have planned on Detective Snyder staying at Mary's house so he will have access to any clues that may have been left behind. He knows more about the case than anyone. He said he has a trusted friend here in our police department. He and Mary had already confided in him, so he should be of help His name is Sheriff Robert Hardy."

"Of course, Preston, whatever you think is best," Whitney said. "I'm a bit in shock. I had no idea all of this was going on. I guess I'm not much of an investigating journalist after all."

"Nonsense. Mary didn't want you involved. She didn't want to put you in any danger. We can go over all the details of the estate after the funeral, If that's all right with you I believe I need to get home now. I need some time alone to sort this all out, as I'm sure you do. Here is the envelope Mary left for you. I'm sure it will answer any questions I may have missed. I will call you tomorrow when I hear from detective Snyder, and we'll arrange to meet. Please call me if there is anything I can do for you. Mary would have wanted me to look after you."

Whitney looked at Preston with tears streaming down her face and hugged him. "What will we do without her?"

Preston couldn't speak and just tipped his hat and walked away.

As soon as the door closed behind Preston, Debbie, who had left the room after delivering coffee to give Preston and Whitney privacy, came into the room.

"Whitney, don't think me unfeeling, but I'm worried that, unknowingly, Mary has placed you right in the frying pan."

"What do you mean?"

"I couldn't help but hear from the kitchen, if this Joshua is as devious as they say, he is going to resent you for getting the family money."

"I never thought of that, but you're probably right, and, indirectly, I could be placing you in danger just by being near me."

"I think we'll be okay, at least until the settling of the estate becomes public knowledge."

"You know, if we can get Preston and Detective Snyder to agree, maybe we could plant a false article in the local paper requesting any knowledge of one Joshua Whitman, whose presence is needed to settle the Whitman estate, blah, blah, blah. It might be a way to draw him out."

"I would like for you to go with me to the meeting when Preston sets it up."

" I'd like to go—that is, if it's okay with the two of you. I know you haven't had time for it to soak in yet, but do you realize how rich you are? I'm not sure you'll want to be associating with us common folk." Debbie said, to lighten the mood a little.

"Would you stop? I don't have a clue how to be rich. I do know that I want to help my parents. They have always been there for me. I probably won't be able to talk Daddy into retiring. He doesn't think of the farm as work. It's a part of life for him. I know one thing I want to do is bring Mom over here. She has always wanted to go someplace out of the country. I think the farthest she has ever been was to Washington, DC, and that was to chaperone Dawn's class trip in ninth grade. She got to take the city tour with a bunch of teenagers, so I'm sure she didn't get much out of that. But she talked about it for months and made two photo albums to commemorate the trip. Aside from that, I can't think about it right now. I guess I can't put off going through Mary's envelope any longer. I am having a hard time realizing that I'll never see her again."

"I tell you what. You go through it, and I'll go fix us some breakfast. If you need me, just holler."

Whitney dumped out the contents of the envelope onto the table. There were several keys tagged as to what they went to, a computer disk and a letter.

When Debbie came back armed with a tray of food, I was still trying to absorb all that had happened in the last few hours.

"Come on, let's eat and talk this out. What are you thinking?"

"I gotta tell you, Deb, I'm having trouble forming one complete thought. I keep skipping around from her poor sister to that trouble with Phillip Fontaine to the possibility of her own nephew killing her."

"Whitney, I just hope you don't think for a minute that you can solve this whole mess and, in some way, avenge Mary's death." Even as she spoke, Debbie could see that curious need that must be in the soul of every writer in Whitney's eyes.

Whitney brought herself back to the present and assured Debbie she would be fine.

Debbie had no doubt in her mind that she might need help in saving Whitney from her need to know the whole story and possibly placing herself right in the thick of things. She suggested that it might be a good idea to alert her family. They needed to hear about Mary's death from her before they heard it on the news. It wouldn't be long before the press picked up on the sensationalism surrounding the death. Mary Whitman was as well known in the States as she was in Europe.

"My mind is whirling. It's as though a major storm is brewing and everything is blowing around and I can't seem to focus on any one thing. I can usually clear a path and concentrate on what's important."

"Whitney, this is probably the strangest, most emotional situation to happen to you personally." replied Debbie.

"Mom and Dad are going to want me to stop everything and jump on a plane and fly home immediately."

"Sorry, but I'm with them! This Joshua sounds like a first-class psycho. If this creep has already murdered to get what he wants, then neither you nor anyone who is close to you is safe."

"I know you're right, but before I can even think about leaving, I have to find out what's on that disk. It might shed some light on all this. It will show me what evidence Mary had compiled."

———#———

CHAPTER 28

If the pounding in his head was any sign, then Joshua Whitman Fontaine has raised more than a few mugs to celebrate his wicked victory. A smug smile spread over his face as he spoke out loud.

"Well, Aunt Mary, it won't be long now until I'll have everything that's rightfully mine. I'm the last heir to the great and powerful Whitman fortune. I'll show them all, I will."

About then, something stirred under the blankets beside him. He'd totally forgotten that he'd not come home alone last night. As she grinned up at him though her rotted teeth, he realized he must have been drunker that he'd thought to have dragged this fine specimen back to his bed.

"Get your ass up and be on your way, bitch."

"You were talking a different tune to me last night, you were."

"I was stinking' drunk last night, and today I can see that you're nothing but a pig and not fit for the likes of me."

"Oh, your lordship, I forgot about the fortune you'll be comin' into, but should I bow before ye?" Sadie Johnson had just sealed her own doom without even knowing it. Joshua must have been bragging to her about the money and God knows what else. Nobody would miss a drunken two-bit whore anyway, and he couldn't take the chance of her not keeping her yap shut.

It was about sundown when the police found Sadie's body down by the riverbank, her throat slit. She hadn't gone without a fight, though. They found blood and skin under her fingernails, and clutched in one hand was an ornate button with a small patch of blue material still clinging to it.

"Well, boys, it looks like this one was done in a hurry. We've at least got some clues to go on."

——⫽——

Dawn was quite shaken after her phone call from Whitney. She wanted to make sure she was calm when she repeated the whole ordeal to her parents. She decided to call and ask Donna and Frank to come over and talk to her about it. Frank was so levelheaded and could maybe give her some advice that would be helpful to Whitney.

When Donna and Frank pulled up, a man was coming out of the barn. As they neared, they saw that it was Kelly Gillespie. He had been a couple years ahead of them in school and was now the vet in Bradleyville. He'd taken over from old man Brewer, who finally had to give up his practice when he mistakenly spayed one of Thelma Middleton's prize breeding dogs when all it was in for was routine shots. He'd been in his nineties and could hardly see but hadn't been ready to give it up.

"Well, look who's here. What's up?" Donna asked.

"Oh, I just heard from Whitney and needed to talk with you guys about something." Dawn said.

"Are you having trouble with some of the animals?" Frank asked.

"Queenie is having trouble foaling, and Kelly may have to reach in and turn it."Dawn said.

Donna introduced Kelly, "HI, Kelly. This is my husband, Frank Kellums."

"I heard around town that you got married. Congratulations, "he said.

Donna inquired, "How's your mom?"

Kelly answered, "She's doin' pretty good. She still misses dad, and I guess she always will."

"How long has it been since he passed away?" Donna asked.

"It's been close to four years now, he replied.

He was a good man. Hey, it was great to see you, but I have an anxious mother in there that needs me. You'll know that feeling soon enough, you and Dawn both."

Frank asked, "Do you need me to help?"

"No, Frank. George is in with her and if need be, he can lend me a hand."

"Let's sit here in the swing. It's such a nice day." After I explained the situation, my own gut feeling had been confirmed. Whitney needed to go as Mary had recommended to her and get out of London until this mess was cleared up. Frank was going to see what he could find out about this Joshua character. We planned to get together at Mom and Dad's and call Whitney. As I suspected, Mom and Dad were worried sick. Mom insisted on making dinner for all of us. Dad said it would keep her mind busy.

"I'm going on home to check my mail, and I'll be back later for some supper with you guys, and then we'll call Whitney." said Frank.

Donna went in the kitchen with mom and as was my daily routine I headed out to the mail-box. Nothing could be done until Frank got back and we could call Whitney.

I was waiting at the mailbox when Kent Gillespie, Kelly's brother and our mail carrier, pulled up to the box.

"I've got something that'll make your day beautiful."

"I'll bet it's from Jimmy then."

"You got it. I think I'd have to worry if a day went by that I didn't see your smiling face here waitin' for your mail."

"Can I get you a soda to take on your travels?"

"No, I'm headin' home. There's fried chicken waitin' for me."

As Kent headed on down the road, I ripped into Jimmy's letter.

Dearest Dawn,

Things are moving along better than we ever imagined. Don't count on it, but we may not need to be here as long as we thought.

It's amazing how well the kids have taken to the school, and there's about four of the locals being trained to take over teaching when we pull out. The gardens are thriving, and it does my heart good to see the look of accomplishment on the people's faces after putting in a hard day's labor. We've set up a machine shop for constructing and repairing the farm equipment.

I haven't told you why Mozambique was our second choice. They are extremely vulnerable to changes brought on by the climate change. Floods and drought nearly cripple farmers' ability to grow crops. We have been teaching them about sustainable irrigation systems and water reservoirs. Up until now, they have had to mostly import fruits, vegetables, and other agricultural products. The actual land is owned by the government, which grants the citizens' rights to the land.

One of the biggest obstacles for us is the language barrier. They speak Portuguese. Thank God we have three members of our group who speak Portuguese and a few locals who speak English. The nuns speak both languages.

It's pretty comfortable weather, usually in the seventies. We've got several fields of hay planted. The government is sending over some cattle to get things started. This week we've putting up fence posts and getting prepared.

Enough about me, how's my favorite girl doing? Have you gotten settled into the cottage? I'm so glad you're there close to family. I know your mom and dad are happy to have you close by, especially since your sister is so far away.

I miss you so much. You don't know how many times I wished I hadn't taken this on, but it has been really fulfilling. I want you to know that I realize not many new wives would have been so understanding. You're one in a million. All my love,

Jimmy

Boy, wouldn't it be wonderful it Jimmy could come home early? I would feel a whole lot better with him to lean on right now.

She told us he was home waiting on an important call, hopefully with some info on Joshua Whitman.

I told them about the possibility that Jimmy might be home earlier than he had expected.

Even though everything was prepared, Mom tried to keep herself busy.

"Mom, you've wiped that same counter at least six times."

"Ida, come and sit with us. If I need to, I'll get myself on one of those jets and go drag our girl home." Then he put his hand over his wife's, and I could see the exchange of looks from one to the other. "I almost forgot to tell you girls. Jessie called just before you got here. She went down to the feed and tack store and ran into an old friend, and they got to talking. It seems this lady's son is a master wood crafter; he has a small shop attached to his house. You know, she's been looking for cribs for the two of you, so she drove over and looked at some of his work. I guess it was just beautiful, so she has this fella making you each a handcrafted cribs."

"Dawn, do you remember the cradles we had for our dolls? I think we were about seven," Donna said.

"Yes," Dawn replied, "Daddy made those for us for Christmas. I can hardly believe that we'll soon be a moms."

When Frank walked in, we were all teary-eyed. "Have you heard something? Is everything okay?"

"Oh, yes, honey. We were just getting sentimental over the birth of these two little sweethearts. Did you get your call?"

"Yes. There's quite a rap sheet on this guy. He should not be taken lightly. Another bit of information: he is quite proficient with disguises. It helps him to slither though right under the noses of officials. I don't want to worry you all more than you are already, but it seems the authorities suspect him of another murder. They found the body of a woman with her throat slit just hours ago. He was a bit careless. They found skin and blood under her nails, and they are checking it against his DNA."

"Daddy, I think you can get through to Whitney better than anyone. You need to make the call to her, and don't take no for an answer."

Daddy must have done what was needed because Whitney could be stubborn. He said she agreed without much arguing.

—— // ——

Whitney knew what she had to do, and she couldn't waste any time. Having her loved ones close by would help. Preston and Detective Snyder made the arrangements, and before she knew it, she and Debbie were on a plane headed to Bradleyville.

"Deb, I just want to tell you how much it means to me that you managed to clear everything so you could be with me. I can't wait 'til you meet my family. They are gonna love you."

"What are you talking about? We're friends. I don't have any family left, so I've decided to be part of yours. Now for the really important question, are you ready to sit back and make the best of a bad situation? Let's drink!"

"I've never traveled in first class, so let the pampering begin. I'll have to sneak a sip of yours since I'm not legal."

"Okay, then I'll be forced to order doubles."

"You're incorrigible, but that's why we get along so well."

After one drink, Debbie struck up a conversation with a junior executive type across the aisle.

Not wanting to be pulled into the conversation, Whitney pretended to be sleeping. The minute her eyes closed, her mind was filled with all the events that had happened in such a short time. The shock, the sadness, and—even though she tried to push it aside—the fear kept washing through her. Finally, out of sheer exhaustion, sleep came, but it wasn't restful. The image of Joshua Fontaine's face kept creeping into her subconscious, all the different faces from all of his disguises, but all of them the same person. He could be anywhere, even on this very plane. Whitney was awakened suddenly by a loud noise. Was it a gun shot? After she woke up more fully, she realized it was just an overhead compartment being shut.

"Whit, it's time to change planes and get some real food."

The next leg of the trip went by quickly, and anticipation of seeing her family kept the horrible images at bay.

The whole family plus Donna and Frank were there to meet the plane.

"Let me look at you two. Are you sure you have two more months to go? You both look ready to deliver now."

"Thanks. You look great too!"

"No, no, you all look beautiful. I just can't believe I'm gonna be an aunt so soon. I can't wait."

"Believe me," said Donna, "we can't wait either."

Ida spoke up. "Let's go home."

—//—

Joshua had been busy; he'd even slipped into Preston's office and picked up enough information to lead him to Whitney. He had obtained fake documents and was on his way to some obscure little bump in the road called Bradleyville. Who were these people anyway, the damned Waltons?

He had researched the backgrounds of the town and specifically the Pracket family. He hit pay dirt when he realized that he had even done business with the late Frank MacIntosh. This would be his ticket in. He would go to the daughter, Donna, and introduce himself as a business acquaintance of her father's.

Fate was on his side, finally!

By the time his work was over, this sleepy little town would know not to underestimate Joshua Whitman Fontaine.

—//—

CHAPTER 29

Preston was arranging for Detective Snyder's son, detective Cody Snyder, to meet with Whitney at her parents' house. He was to arrive later that day. He would be coordinating the case with his father, handling things from London while he took care of business in Bradleyville.

When Whitney finally woke up, Debbie's bed was already made. She went down and found her mother in the kitchen making her favorite pie.

"Hey, Ma, have you seen Debbie?"

"She is out helping your dad. She said she'd never been on a farm and asked your dad if she could go with him." Mom started to laugh. "You should have seen her."

"What's so funny?"

"Well, she came down in a pretty little outfit, so Bob got her a pair of your old overalls and some work boots. I thought maybe she'd back out, but all she said was, "Don't I get a straw hat to go with this? "You'd have thought she was about to go to the circus. I like her. I'm glad she's been there for you through all this."

"She's helping Dad?"

Her mother shrugged and went on with her baking but kept her eyes on her daughter. Whitney knew her well enough to know she wanted to talk.

"I'm so sorry about Mary. I know how close you two were."

"Mom, there's something I haven't explained. I know you know that Mary left me money, but I haven't told you how much she left me. Even with all that money, I would rather have Mary alive. I'll never get to learn all that she had to teach me, which is priceless. She said she thought of me as the daughter, she never had." said Whitney with tears in her eyes.

"It doesn't really matter, honey. I just think it was so good of her to name you in her will at all." Mom said.

"Mom, I am a very rich woman! I've never been rich before, but it's sad to have it happen like this." Whitney replied.

Hearing that, Ida plopped down in a chair with a stunned look. "How rich are you?"

"Let's just say there is a mansion in London that you will be staying in whenever you want, and you will only be flying first class. You and Dad don't have to work another day in your lives. You can finally travel to all the places you always wanted to go to. I have already spoke with Jimmy's Professor Higgins and pledged a substantial amount of money to his project with the understanding that it was to enable Jimmy to get home as soon as possible!" She had taken him into her confidence about her sister's pregnancy and the other drama that was unfolding. He swore not to mention it to Jimmy. Whitney didn't want to jeopardize the project nor Jimmy's dreams, so whatever they needed, she was willing to pay.

Then Whitney seemed sad again. "If I could choose to be rich or have Mary alive, I would not have to think for even a second, but it wasn't left up to me. Mary specified that she knew I would help my family, so please talk to Daddy, and don't you dare let him keep working so hard. You both deserve some frivolous fun in your life. It would make me so happy to know that all this helped those I love. How am I going to finish Mary's book?"

Ida had tears in her eyes, hugged her daughter, and then pulled away and looked in her eyes. "Honey, this is your money. We can't spend it."

"Oh, Mom, there's more money than I could spend in two lifetimes. I want to help Dawn and Jimmy, too, if Jimmy's not too stubborn. I even pledged the money for his program with the understanding that he would not know who gave it. I wanted you to know so you wouldn't worry about Dawn being alone during her last few months of pregnancy. You can tell Daddy, but no one else. Of course, the money will not all be available until all the legal process is finished. Preston and Detective Bud Snyder have managed to place an article in the papers saying that the reading of the will has been delayed until they decide the cause of death and until they find Mary's next of kin. They are trying to steer Joshua Fontaine away from me and to lure him to contact them.

I just hope and pray that I haven't brought any danger to all of you."

"Whitney Pracket, you are home with people who love you, and we're not going to let anyone hurt any of our family. Donna's Frank has already been a big help, and this young Detective Cody Snyder will be here. We will stand together and protect our own. That slimeball Fontaine doesn't know who he's messin' with!"

"Mama, I've never heard you talk like this."

"I've never needed to until now."

Whitney announced that she needed some alone time, and she went to her room and laid on her bed and staired at the ceiling, thinking about the next steps for the book.

She went to her desk and made a diagram of information she had gathered, information on Mary's computer and what sources she still needed to contact.

She decided to put on her journalist hat and move forward as soon as possible. This pesky business of someone wanting to possibly kill her needed to be taken care of first.

Whitney decided to go downstairs with Ida and wait for Debbie to come back.

A few hours later, Bob and Debbie came to the kitchen door—or it sort of looked like Debbie.

"What happened to you?"

Bob and Debbie were laughing so hard they couldn't speak. Finally, Bob managed to talk about how Debbie thought it would be a good idea to give Mabel, the very pregnant sow, a bath and rub down.

"Mabel had other ideas. I'm not sure which one looks worse."

"Quit, I'm gonna pee my pants, and I can't come in like this." She was laughing so hard she nearly doubled over. Ida led her to the mudroom and brought her a robe so she could go take a shower.

Bob and Whitney waited in the kitchen. He was still laughing.

"I'm glad you brought Debbie. She's quite a character."

"I'm glad you like her. We haven't known each other that long, but we are as close as if we'd grown up together." "Debbie doesn't have any family living, and I think she needs us to be her family." Bob nodded in agreement.

"When is that detective supposed to be here?"

"I'm not really sure. Sometime this evening."

Arrangements had been made for Cody Snyder to stay at Frank and Donna's. He was to be introduced around town as Cody Wyatt, a friend of Frank's from college.

CHAPTER 30

Another arrival in Bradleyville went without much notice as he checked into the local hotel. An elderly man of about seventy with white hair and a beard, walking with the aid of a cane, was checked into room fifty-six at the Creekside Lodge.

Carrie Hawk, one of Bradleyville's chief gossips, had been at the front desk. Carrie made it her business to know a little bit about everything that went on in town. When she passed it on, usually at the Beauty Spot while under the dryer, it sometimes changed just enough to catch the attention of whoever happened to be under the dryer next to her.

Business had been slow, so she was elated at the possibility of something new to pass along at her usual appointment the following day.

Back at the Creekside Lodge Joshua Fontaine AKA Ryan Matthews was checking in.

"How long do you plan to be with us, Mr. Matthews?"

"My dear, I'm not quite sure. I'm here to pay my respects to someone I've not actually met before."

"I know about everyone in town. Maybe I could be of some help to you. Who is it you're here to see?"

"Donna MacIntosh Kellums. She was the daughter of a man I knew many years ago."

"I know Donna, but this town is not too fond of the late Frank MacIntosh." Carrie said.

"Why?" asked Fontaine, AKA Matthews.

"There was a time when he was the envy of every businessman in town, everything he touched seemed to turn to gold, but we don't take to kindly to crooks around here. I hope you weren't one of the people he took advantage of."

"No, I knew him only briefly, and I assure you, he didn't cheat me."

"I hope you enjoy your stay, and if I can be of help in any way, please don't hesitate to let me know. Henry will show you to your room."

Once safely behind closed doors, Joshua looked at himself in the mirror and admired his new persona of Ryan Matthews, an elderly gentleman from Florida. He had counted on the nosy desk clerk to test his new identity on, and it had worked like a charm. These ignorant little people would be putty in his hands.

He liked the thought of using a friend to get to that little know-nothing bitch that Mary had given his inheritance to. Just thinking about doing away with her gave him a high.

He would infiltrate himself into the Kellums' home, and that would eventually lead him to her.

———//———

CHAPTER 31

They had just finished supper when the doorbell rang at the Pracket house. Whitney answered the door, and standing there was a man dressed in jeans, a chambray shirt, and boots. He had piercing blue eyes. Whitney suddenly went mute until he flashed a sexy smile and said, "I believe you're expecting me, I'm Cody Snyder."

Feeling just a little foolish at her sudden loss of the ability to speak, Whitney stepped back to put a little distance between them and said, "Yes, please come in, detective."

"Please call me Cody." There was that smile again.

When they were all introduced and seated in the living room, Debbie sidled over beside Whitney and whispered, "I guess you won't mind having this gorgeous man looking out for you?"

"I hadn't noticed."

"Right! That's why you suddenly lost your voice."

"I...Oh, shut up."

The news Cody had for them caused them all to shut up!

"We have reason to believe that Fontaine is either here in town already or on his way. There was a break-in at Preston's office. Nothing was taken, but his files were strewn around and some of his computer data had been copied."

Ida was obviously shaken, and asked

"What are you going to do to keep my daughter safe?"

Bob tried to console her, but it was Cody who knelt beside her and assured her that Whitney would not be out of his sight.

Whitney spoke up, a bit shaken herself. "Is that entirely necessary? What about your cover and you staying at Frank and Donna's?"

Looking directly into Whitney's eyes, he gave her that look that did something funny to her insides. "I think between all of us we can come up with a viable cover that will allow me to stay here near you."

Debbie offered what everyone, but Whitney thought it was a perfect solution. She suggested that Cody could pretend to be her fiancé. Cody agreed that being engaged would explain them being together all the time if Whitney could do her part and pretend to be in love with him.

Ida got a room ready for Cody, and he was getting settled in. Whitney was in her room pacing the floor.

"This is never going to work. He's not my type."

"Well, girl, you certainly seem to be his type."

"What on earth are you talking about?"

"Oh please, I've seen the sparks shoot between both of you when you look at each other. Never mind any of that. What counts is that the two of you can pull off this charade. It could mean the difference in life and death."

"I guess I haven't been thinking about the danger aspect. I'm placing Cody in danger as well as myself. I am going to do whatever it takes for all of us to get through this."

Dawn was beginning to feel totally exhausted from all the excitement of the last few days.

"Today I am not going to do anything but lie around in my pajamas and veg out."

Just as Dawn started streaming one of her favorite Streisand movies, *The Mirror Has Two Faces*, the phone rang.

"Do I get it or ignore it? Oh, crap if I don't get it and it's Mom, she'll just come down here. Okay, I'll get it. Hello? Hey, Donna, what's up?"

"Well, I just got the strangest call. A Mr. Ryan Matthews—he knew my dad several years ago and he wants to stop by to pay his respects."

Do you think he and your dad were involved in anything illegal?"

"I have absolutely no idea."

"Don't you dare agree to meet him alone. You make sure Frank is there."

"I already invited him to come over tomorrow for Sunday dinner. He said he's staying at the Creekside Lodge. Frank thought he'd stop by and chat with Carrie. You know she loves nothing better than to tell everything she knows and then some. What are you doing today? You sound kind of tired."

"I am, so I've decided to lie around and be a slob."

"Okay, I'll let you go since you have the perfect plan."

"Please let me know how your dinner turns out."

"Okay, get some rest, and I'll be in touch."

———//———

Joshua's plan was set in motion. Now for step two.

———//———

Whitney was going stir-crazy. Mom was afraid for her to go out of the house, and Dad was always busy with one thing or the other on the farm. Dawn hadn't even been by.

Cody had brought some elaborate computer system with him, and Debbie was helping him set it up in the guest room.

Whitney decided she'd been shut in long enough. She got dressed and even made it to the car when she realized the damn keys were on her dresser. Determined to make her break, she quietly went back in the house, retrieved her keys, and was at the door. When she opened it, there Cody was.

"Going somewhere without me, darling?"

"As a matter of fact, yes. I'm going to town."

"I guess I could check around town and see if anything unusual is going on."

"Not exactly what I had in mind," said Whitney, "but if you're going with me, you'd better get a coat and hurry up."

"I just love it when you boss me around. It's almost as if we're an old married couple already. Ha!"

The drive into town was made in silence, but before they got out of the car, Cody took hold of Whitney's arm, and there it was, that weird feeling deep in the pit of her stomach. She couldn't be attracted to him. She didn't even like him. Oh, he was smooth, all right, but in a cocky, macho kind of way. She wouldn't give him the satisfaction of knowing he had any effect on her other than pure annoyance. She turned and glared at him.

"What do you want now?"

"Debbie told me that you were prepared to do your part and act like we were a loving couple. You need to stop being a spoiled brat and go along with this. You could be placing all of us in danger." There definitely was no smile in his eyes when he spoke this time. "Either we do this my way, or we go back home."

"Mr. Snyder, I would never put anyone in danger, and when in public, I will appear to be the devoted fiancé. But when we're alone, don't ever touch me or lecture me again."

"No problem, sweetheart. You're hardly my type anyway."

Whitney was livid inside, but she flashed Cody a sweet smile, took his hand, and led him toward the Beauty Spot, where she hoped Cody would feel extremely out of place. When they walked in, Cody looked around. The walls were bright pink, and white frilly priscilla curtains hung at each window. There were four stylist chairs with ladies in different stages of haircuts, color, and comb-outs. He couldn't figure out how the ones under the dome-shaped dryers ever managed to dry their hair since, for the most part, they were leaned over to their neighbor, obviously spreading the news that, no doubt, you wouldn't find in the local newspaper.

An attractive woman, probably in her late twenties, ran over and hugged Whitney.

"I heard you were home. It seems like forever since I first cut your hair!"

"Yeah, I just hope you don't still use pinking shears!" Whitney laughed.

"You can ask Emily. It's been at least fifteen years. I believe you were five, and I was around thirteen."

Emily just grinned and shook her head as she applied what looked like blue whipped cream to the little old lady in her chair.

"Who is this gorgeous man, Whit?"

"Sarah Webster, this is my fiancé, Cody Wyatt. Cody, darling, this is my cousin Sarah, and over there is her sister and my cousin, Emily."

Then all three of them were hugging and jumping up and down like three little schoolchildren.

"I can't believe it. You're getting married? I hope the wedding will be here in town; we'll close the shop for the day and do all the hair. You just let us know when you set the date."

"This isn't just a social visit. So, do either of you have time to make a new woman out of me? And I think Cody could use a trim. Couldn't you, honey?" Whitney had that cat-swallowing-the-canary look on her face, hoping that Mr. Snyder/ Wyatt would retreat to snoop around and leave her alone for a while. Maybe she could shake this feeling she had every time he was around her. Of course it wasn't to be, because the next thing she heard, he was looking at her with a body-melting smile saying, "I'd feel honored to have one of these lovely ladies work their magic on me."

He had definitely won them over. Damn! He was incorrigible. Did nothing ruffle him?

By the time they left the Beauty Spot, he not only looked even more handsome than ever, but he had talked to each and every one of the women there. By the looks on their faces, the whole town would know about the charming Cody Wyatt before the end of the day.

"I'm starving," he said. "Could we get something to eat before we head back to your parents' house? You do realize that I'm not the enemy, don't you?"

"I know, and I'm sorry if I've given you attitude."

"If?"

"Okay, let's go into Herley's and have lunch."

"Maybe we could even talk. After all we're engaged, and we should know something about each other. Deal?"

"I've been coming in here since I was a little girl. It has always been the local hangout. Back when my parents were in high school, they came here too. It brings back so many memories. Mom told me this is where Dad first asked her to go steady."

Cody felt his resolve weakening as he looked at Whitney with that sweet, dreamy expression on her face. He knew better than to fall for a client. He wasn't afraid of this Joshua character, but Whitney Pracket scared him to death.

—#—

As they walked into the kitchen, Whitney could tell her mother was upset about something.

"What's up, Mom?"

"It's Dawn. She's not feeling well."

"Oh no, is she going to be okay?"

"The doctor said she just needed to stay off her feet for a while. I'll go stay with her and take care of her. Who's with her now, Dad?"

"No, Debbie volunteered. We thought since you're probably the target of that lunatic, you might inadvertently draw danger to your sister."

It finally all came down on Whitney, and she ran from the room in tears. Cody started to go after her, but Ida said, "I'll go, I've probably handled more female tears than you have, and I'm sure she wouldn't want you to see her like this."

As he looked out the kitchen window, he saw mother and daughter sobbing together and hugging each other, and his heart melted. This family was getting to him. He made a mental note to call his dad. He rarely saw him. Even though they were in the same line of work, they rarely worked on the same case. His mom had died when he was fourteen, but he still missed her and the love that only a mother could give. His dad had done the best he could, but dads seem to have more trouble showing their love, especially to their sons, and sons don't ever want to appear vulnerable in front of another male, even if it is their dad. For a long time, he'd avoided what he really wanted to do in life because it was the same line of work that his dad did, but since he had decided to quit fighting it, they got along better than ever. They had developed a mutual respect for each other and finally shared a common goal.

Cody knew that his dad had a personal interest in this case, so that made it even more crucial that he catch this Fontaine creep.

The phone rang, and since no one else was in the house, Cody answered, "Hello, this is Cody. What have you gotten so far? I can come right now and pick it up. Thanks for working so quickly, Chief Hackney."

He wanted to let Whitney and Ida know where he'd be and to make sure Whitney wouldn't be alone while he was gone.

He approached the two women cautiously, not wanting to intrude on anything. Whitney looked a little pale and flushed from crying, and the thoughts that were going through his mind had nothing to do with the case and everything to do with touching her and feeling her against him.

My god, man. Get it together, he thought. Her mother is right there.

As if she could tell what he had been thinking just by looking at him, they both looked at him waiting for him to speak.

Ida broke the silence. "Cody, is something wrong?"

"No, I'm sorry to interrupt, but Chief Hackney just called, and he has a list compiled for me, with the names of any people who have arrived in town in the last few days and where they are staying. He even knows the purpose of some of their visits. I am going to run down to the police station and pick it up, and I wanted to make sure everything was okay and ask if the two of you would mind staying in the house while I'm away. Whitney, I know you're upset over your sister, but you can't blame yourself. How about you give her a call and see if she would mind the two of us coming over tomorrow for a short visit? Maybe if you can physically see her, you'll feel better." He saw the corners of her mouth start to form a smile, and she came over to him and hugged him.

"Detective Snyder, you're not all bad. Thanks."

As he was driving away from the Prackets', he was thankful that it had been a brief hug since Ida had been standing beside them. If she had lingered, he might have embarrassed them all.

Whitney was relieved to see for herself that Dawn was obeying her doctor and seemed to be feeling better. She thought about telling her about Jimmy coming home, but if something went wrong, it would be devastating for her.

It was amazing how everyone reacted to Cody. It was as if he had always been in their lives. In the midst of the conversation going on around them, Whitney and Cody's eyes met and locked on each other, their heartbeats quickened, and each of them knew without a word being spoken that something had changed between them. What broke into the moment was a name that brought Cody back to reality—Ryan Matthews!

"What did you say about Ryan Matthews?"

Dawn repeated the conversation she had had with Donna. Cody was instantly on guard. "It's him!"

"Do you know this man?"

"Not Ryan Matthews, but I do know Joshua Fontaine, and I'd be willing to bet my career that they are one and the same. You say this dinner is tonight?"

"Yes, he's expected at around 7:00 p.m."

"What should we do?"

"We need to worn Donna."

Detective Cody Snyder went to see if Donna and Frank were willing to go along with his plan. He told them about his suspicion that Ryan Matthews was in fact Joshua Fontaine.

He briefed them about his plan, and they both agreed to play their parts. They said they would do anything to help get this dangerous man brought to justice.

I have a plan, but I need all of you to help me with it."

Donna was a nervous wreck and just a little bit intrigued to be a part of the scam that was going to happen in her very own home.

Cody had worked like a magician to get the FBI agents to play servants at the Kellums' house for the night. This guy was going to be toast!

Promptly at 7:00 p.m., a cab pulled up, and a man who appeared to be in his sixties got out and was coming toward the door.

Joshua couldn't help but be impressed by the three-story Victorian as he approached. His plan was to worm information out of the close friend and neighbor of precious Whitney Pracket, darling of Aunt Mary and the little bitch who had what was rightfully his.

He was greeted at the door by a butler. This was the kind of life that should be his. Okay, it was time to get into character.

He was led into the living room and presented to Mr. and Mrs. Kellums.It was obvious that Matthews, or whoever he was, had known Daddy, he talked about business, that my dad had helped him with. He said that together they had bought a large parcel of land meant to go to the state for low income housing, and developed it, building high end Condos. He oozed con artist.

The bell rang again, and Donna announced to Kaedan, the butler, "That's probably Whitney and Cody. Please show them in. Mr. Matthews, I hope you don't mind, but I invited a close friend and her fiancé to join us. Whitney is also our neighbor, and she's just recently gotten back from London."

"Why, no, my dear. The more the merrier I always say."

Introductions were made, and Kaedan came in to announce that dinner was ready to be served.

The dinner conversation flowed smoothly, and Donna asked Whitney how Dawn was feeling. Whitney told Donna that she wasn't doing too well.

"I'll be going over tomorrow to take my turn staying with her. She insists on staying at the cottage, so Mom and Dad and all of us are taking turns spending the night there."

Cody leaned over and gave Whitney a quick kiss on the cheek. "You will be missed."

Whitney blushed.

Kaedan came in to clear some of the glasses and serve more wine.

Frank looked at Whitney with such sympathy in his eyes. "I'm so sorry your family has had to go through so much stress and sadness lately. I don't know if you're aware of any of this, Mr. Matthews, but Whitney worked with Mary Whitman, the international journalist who was murdered recently in London?"

"Oh my, I had no idea, and your poor sister is expecting and ill? Where is the poor dear's husband?"

"Jimmy is in Mozambique heading up a government project to help educate the people in agricultural areas, as well as setting up schools and day care centers. He hopes to train several of the local people so that they can take over when he comes home," Cody offered. He went on praising the project, telling more in depth of what Jimmy and his group had carried out.

Whitney sat spellbound. She didn't even know as much as he did about a member of her own family. He had related the story with such passion that she almost forgot that they were breaking bread with a possible murderer.

Joshua Fontaine, by appearances, was totally absorbed in Cody's story, but inside his twisted mind, he was already planning how to take out his next roadblock to his fortune.

Everyone was a bit surprised at his arrogance when he turned the conversation back around to the murder in London.

"I certainly hope they apprehended the murderer of your friend and coworker," he said.

"No, I'm afraid they haven't," Whitney said with a genuine catch in her voice as she fought back tears that burned at her eyes. Mary had been her mentor and very dear friend, and she missed her so much.

Donna could see how emotional this was for Whitney and changed the subject by inviting everyone into the living room for coffee and dessert.

As they sat comfortably sipping coffee and chatting, Kaedan put Matthews's glass into an evidence bag to be dropped off at Sheriff Hackney's office to verify his identity against fingerprints on file for Joshua Fontaine.

Ryan Matthews thanked his hosts and bid everyone farewell and left.

The first part of the plot to capture Fontaine had gone well. While they had all been at Donna and Frank's sharing dinner with the enemy, agents had been preparing for tomorrow's ambush. Surveillance equipment and listening devices had been placed in the cottage, and two female agents were there posing as Dawn and Whitney. One of the agents was Olivia Hobbs, who looked like Whitney. The other, Camela Latsha, posing as Dawn, even wore a pregnant belly pad strapped under her clothing. They would be staying the night at the cottage tonight just in case Fontaine decided to check it out before tomorrow.

Sheriff Hackney called Cody on his cell phone to let him know everything was in place.

During dinner, Donna had made a point of asking Whitney to come by around five before she went to Dawn's because she wanted to prepare their dinner to help. Of course, this was just to make sure Fontaine knew when to expect Whitney to be at the cottage.

Since Fontaine had been at the Creekside Lodge, he had been keenly aware of the comings and goings of the lodge. He knew that no one would notice him leaving in the wee hours of the morning. So around 3:00 a.m., he crept down the stairs and out a back door that he had managed to get the keys to. He indeed wanted to scout out the area around the cottage. He took a duffel bag packed with his expensive new identity, airline tickets, and all pertinent or incriminating items, and stashed it in a locker at the train station at the edge of town. He would assume his new identity along with a new disguise and slip out of town just as easily as he had slipped into town as soon as the job was done.

Imagine his luck at being in the right place at the right time. The sniveling little fool sitting next to him at that dive of a bar last night was more than willing to spill his guts about being fired. Normally he would have let the man know that he didn't give a damn, but as it turned out, he was the sheriff's nephew and was mad as hell about some big deal going on at the sheriff's office that they didn't want him involved in.

"That bastard detective, Cody Snyder, I told him what I thought of him. Then," he slurred, "my fat-ass uncle got in my face and told me I wouldn't even have a job if my mom wasn't pestering him. I hope Joshua Fontaine gives them the slip."

How ironic that it was the sheriff's nephew, Kolton, who had told him about the fingerprints.

He'd have to pay a visit to the local yokel tomorrow and intercept that report before it got to Detective Snyder. The stupid nephew was drunk enough to put himself out of commission, but just as a little insurance, Fontaine put an extra whammy in his beer to make sure he stayed out for the day. After taking the keys, he could let himself into the sheriff's office bright and early before Hackney showed up.

The basement of the sheriff's office had provided an adequate hiding place until he could catch the old man alone.

Hackney was looking over the reports on the fingerprints, so absorbed that he didn't realize that someone was coming up behind him until his head was jerked back and a knife was at his throat.

Cody answered his cell phone, noting that it was the sheriff's office.

"Hello," Hackney said. "Hardy's not our man, and the fingerprints don't match."

"That's not possible," Cody said through his teeth. "I'm coming down there to look them over myself."

Cody alerted everyone to the possibility that tonight's plan was on hold until they heard from him.

Ten minutes after Cody left, a delivery truck pulled up to deliver flowers to Whitney.

"Who would be sending me flowers?" said Whitney. She tried to keep her expression from showing fear as she read the card attached.

If you want to protect your family, you'll go to your sister's cottage as planned. It's you I want. No one else needs to be hurt.

Mom was standing anxiously nearby, wanting to know who sent her flowers.

Thinking quickly, Whitney replied, "Cody sent me flowers to thank me for my help last night."

"He is so considerate and sweet."

Whitney quickly put the card in her pocket. "Mom, I think I'll ride Queenie out and let Dad know what's going on."

"Do you think that's a good idea?" Ida said in concern.

Whitney was so scared, but she was not going to put her family in danger because of her. She knew where her dad kept a gun in the barn to use to get rid of coyotes. He had taught her and Dawn how to shoot when they were in their early teens. Whitney never imagined needing to use it on a human.

—#—

CHAPTER 32

It didn't appear that anyone was in the office when Cody arrived. Damn, he had been so sure that Matthews and Fontaine were one and the same.

When he saw the reports lying open on the desk, he walked over and that's when he saw the blood. Hackney was lying there in a pool of blood with his throat slit.

"Oh my god!"

Cody quickly called the agents who had been stationed at the cottage. No answer. That wasn't good. His thoughts at once went to Whitney.

He checked the listening device that was to monitor conversation from the cottage. It had been disconnected. He hooked it back up, but there was no sound. He ran to his car and dialed the Pracket house as he was pulling away.

Debbie answered, "Hello?"

"Where is Whitney?" he asked frantically.

"My god, Cody, she's taken her horse and said she was going to tell her daddy that Matthews isn't Joshua. What's going on?"

"All I can tell you is lock the doors and windows. I'm sending some agents over there right now. Don't let anyone leave the house. I'm going after Whitney."

Whitney knew she was walking into a trap, but she was the one who brought this predator near to her family.

When she rode up to the cottage, she saw the door standing open but no signs of anyone around. The only agent that should still be there was Camela Latsha. She went inside and saw the girl's body lying on the floor. She looked totally lifeless. She moved over to check her pulse. Thankfully, she detected a pulse, but she was out cold. Before Whitney could try to revive her, she heard a noise from behind her. She jumped up, and when she turned around, there he was, but not in the persona of Ryan Matthews, He was himself, Joshua Fontaine.

"Well, we meet at last," he said.

She was indeed facing the devil, and there was no mistaking his intentions. She could see death in his eyes!

"Where's your pretend fiancé now?"

"I'm sure you already know. What did you do to Sheriff Hackney to get him to make that call?"

At that moment, he held up a large knife and ran his fingers along its blade. "I'm afraid I had to dispose of him. He wasn't at all cooperative after the phone call."

Whitney felt herself trembling and was afraid her legs would give out on her at any minute.

Fontaine had his back to the door, and just as he was about to lunge at Whitney, he saw her glance up in surprise as if someone was behind him.

"You can't pull that stale trick on me." Then he whirled around when he heard, "Oh, but she can!"

It was Jimmy! The two men struggled. Fontaine still had the knife, and it looked as if he had the upper hand when all of a sudden Whitney heard a gunshot. At first, she didn't know who had been hit or how until she heard Camela and saw Fontaine fall to the floor.

"Thank god you regained consciousness; I didn't know what to do."

All Cody heard when he pulled into the driveway was a gunshot. He was in the cottage in seconds. He saw a man he'd never seen before holding Whitney and comforting her, Agent Latsha with a gun in her hand and holding her head, and a dead body.

When Whitney saw him, she ran into his arms.

Jimmy tried to help Camela get into a chair, then looked at Cody, and said, "I'm Jimmy Connors, Dawn's husband. This is not exactly the homecoming I had expected. Could someone tell me where my wife is?"

"Oh, Jimmy, I'm so glad you're home. You have a lot of surprises ahead of you. Dawn is at Mom and Dad's."

———//———

It had been six weeks since the excitement and tragedy in Bradleyville.

Donna and Frank had a healthy, happy baby girl. They named her Riley Ann Kellums.

Jimmy and Dawn were inseparable. They didn't have much longer until their little one would arrive.

The most surprising thing to happen was Mom and Dad agreeing to go to London to tie up some loose ends for Whitney concerning the estate. Whitney had just put them on a plane to London this morning.

Jimmy had become good friends with a man involved in his project in Mozambique, and he had shown up about a week after Jimmy. Duffy could do anything. He had been helping Dad around the farm. He had grown up on a farm in Indiana, but he'd lost both of his parents to cancer several years ago. He had three sisters and two brothers scattered around the States that he rarely saw. He had fallen for Bradleyville from all Jimmy's stories and wanted to check it out himself.

Dad had felt comfortable leaving since Duffy had agreed to be in charge of the farm for him. Even though Dad had been a bit apprehensive about leaving, he didn't want to disappoint Mom. Preston had agreed to be their guide while they were staying in the Whitman mansion. Whitney had to giggle when she thought of her mother in a house with servants. She'd have the cook making fried chicken and milk gravy in less than a week.

Debbie had fallen in love with country life and was trying to figure out how she could manage to move here. She had been great with computers but was a bit burned out, so she was considering a total change. There had been a connection between her and Duffy. They fought all the time, but it was that electric kind between two strong-willed people who didn't want to acknowledge their attraction to each other. It was almost like a mating ritual and very entertaining to watch.

The loneliness came over Whitney as she thought of Cody, who had been gone since the day after that horrible night with Joshua Fontaine.

"This is just plain silly," Whitney said to herself. "I wasn't really married to him, and I only knew him for a little over a week, not nearly long enough to feel this alone without him."

All around her were couples. It seemed like everyone besides her had someone to comfort them, someone to have fun with, and someone who loved her. She should feel great. The fear and anxiety over catching Mary's murderer was over and she had more money than she knew what to do with, but something was missing.

The decision to buy the hometown newspaper, the *Bradleyville Times*, was a good one. It may not have the excitement and glamour of being an international journalist, but after all that had happened, she had learned something from Mary. She could still do what she loved and have a life, a life that included family and friends and home. She could still travel, and since she'd decided to keep Mary's house in London, the whole family could use it.

Then it was as if Mary were speaking to her from beyond: "Darlin' girl, I've taught you better than to sit around feeling sorry for yourself. If there is something you want out of life, you go out and grab it. I always told you, you can do anything you set your mind to."

It seemed as though Mary was still looking out for her, and knowing Mary as she did, she'd better get her act together and quit wasting time on idle self-pity.

She was giving a very important baby shower today at Donna's, and she was not about to cause her sister anything but happiness and joy.

It wasn't just a baby shower, but a kind of reunion of sorts. Patsey and Matt, now engaged, would be there. Jessie, who'd come to help Donna with the baby and to see Jimmy, had insisted on doing all the cooking. Julie would be there as long as none of her patients went into labor.

It had been a hard choice for Mom and Dad to leave, knowing about the shower and that Dawn might have her baby while they were away, but there were things in London that needed tending to, and they decided that since Duffy was available and Whitney needed to get to work at the paper, now was the best possible time to go. Whitney had to also finish Mary's book. It was important to her to do this not only for Mary but also to expose the corruption.

Whitney had wanted to help Dawn and Jimmy get a bigger house, but Dawn wouldn't hear of it. She loved her cottage, so they decided to add on to the existing house.

Whitney had been looking at a few houses for herself but hadn't been able to decide on one yet. It wasn't like she had to be in a hurry. Besides, right now she has two house guests, Debbie and Duffy.

When Whitney arrived at Donna's, she was amazed at how well everything had come together. The house looked spectacular, filled with flowers and the typical baby shower decorations, but what was heavenly were the delicious smells coming from the kitchen.

Whitney followed the wonderful smells and said "Jessie, you have outdone yourself. No one will leave here today hungry, that's for sure."

Jessie blushed at Whitney's compliment. "You can't know what a labor of love this has been for me. My son is home safe with his wife, and one grandbaby and another one due anytime, I have never felt more blessed."

"Speaking of grandbabies, where are Donna and Riley?"

"Donna's upstairs bathing Riley and dressing her for the party."

"What can I do to help?"

"Nothing, dear. It's all ready. Why don't we sit and have a cup of coffee or a glass of wine? Which do you prefer?"

"I'd love a glass of wine, thanks."

Everyone had a great time at the shower. It was like old home week, seeing some of their friends for the first time in so long. Julie nearly made it through the whole party before she finally got beeped.

The party had dwindled down to family and Debbie and Duffy. They were all sitting out back around the pool, catching up on all that had been going on in everyone's lives.

The doorbell rang, and Frank went to see who it was. When he walked back out to the patio, everyone quit talking, and then they looked up and then at Whitney, whose back had been to Frank.

"What?" Then she turned around and looked directly into Cody's eyes. She felt like they were the only two people there. She had decided that if she had the opportunity, she wasn't going to let him wonder how she felt. She boldly walked over to him, took his face in her hands, and gave him the kiss of his life. His arms went around her and held on. Neither one wanted this moment to end, but since they had an audience, they would have to finish this later.

Cody turned to everyone and said, "I hope you don't mind, but I brought someone who wanted to meet all of you." Then he turned to the man behind him and said, "This is my father, detective Bud Snyder. He came to help me set up my new office.

Whitney looked at him questioningly. "Your office?"

"Yes, ma'am. I'm proud to say I'm the new sheriff." He looked at Whitney. "Could I see you alone for a few minutes?"

"Sure," she said, dumbfounded by the news.

"So, I hear you bought the *Bradleyville Times*?"

"Yes, I decided that it's important to me to be around the people I love." "It doesn't look too good that the new owner and editor didn't even have a clue about your news."

"Do you think you can fit one more person into that group?" Cody said.

"What group?" Whitney replied questioningly.

"The group of people you love?" Cody said, smiling from ear to ear.

She blushed. "Why, sheriff, what are you asking me?"

"I know we haven't known each other long, but I know that I want to get to know you better and see where this goes. I love you, Whitney Pracket."

"I love you more, Cody Snyder."

"So, are you in for the ride of your life with me?" asked Cody.

"That is a definite yes." Whitney said.

CHAPTER 33

Finally, the day had come, Dawn's water broke, and Jimmy was a nervous wreck. Whitney and Debbie told him to just get Dawn to the hospital and they would let Julie know, grab Dawn's bag and meet him there.

Dawn had been prepped and Julie came into the room ready to bring a new life into the world.

It was a normal labor process, at least for Dawn, but Jimmy looked like he'd been drug through a knothole.

Then with the last push baby, Madison Rain McCoy was welcomed to the family.

She was beautiful, she had red hair, weighed seven pounds eight ounces. She also had a set of lungs that let everyone know she had arrived.

Out in the waiting room were; Jessie, Whitney, Debbie, Patsey, Donna and Frank. Duffy was busy at the farm and Cody was tracking down a cattle rustler, who had hit four ranches already.

They were all awaiting the news when Jimmy came out with the precious bundle wrapped in a pink blanket. Everyone was trying to get a look and there were a lot of ooh's and ah's and a few happy tears from Nana Jessie.

The proud parents couldn't wait to get their daughter home to the cottage and start their lives together.

Jimmy had been elected to be the president of the local Farmers Co-op. He also was still helping people anywhere in the world, virtually, to learn proper techniques and stay on track with their farming and ranching. He got paid from several colleges to do this virtual teaching.

CHAPTER THIRTY-FOUR

Cody and Whitney were thinking of moving in together. Whitney had bought a big house near downtown. It was close to her work and to the sheriff's office. Cody was in a small efficiency apartment above the hardware store.

They were so entertaining to watch. If you didn't know them, you would think they were in serious relationship trouble. They are so much alike and each one of them needs to be right. The best part is in the middle of some of their spats, their eyes locked and they grab each other and kiss long and hard, and then it's all calm.

Patsey had changed her major to nursing so she and Matt could work together.

Matt had gone out on his own and opened an office in Monroe. They were developing their relationship and were both happy.

Donna and Frank had decided to get started on baby number two, and they were looking into adopting a child a little older from the adoption agency in Mozambique where Jimmy had been. Jimmy had some contacts, so the ball was rolling on that.

Donna now had a family full of love.

Ida and Bob Pracket are spending half their time in Bradleyville and the other half traveling.

Ida is finally getting to live her dream and now also loves being on their farm and being around family. Bob still prefers the farm but is happy to see his wife so happy and fulfilled.

Julie Beaumont has started dating Kelly Gillespie, the local veterinarian, who knows what will come of that.

There have been so many highs and lows for all of them over this past couple of years, but they made it through with the love and help that only a small town provides.

Who could have imagined that past year and a half? I, Dawn Pracket, leaving the comfort of home, going to college, meeting Patsey, Jimmy, and Donna's mother.

Falling in love, becoming a mom. Speaking of love, all the couples that formed and joined our family.

The End

ABOUT THE AUTHOR

I am married and had 5 children. I was born in a small town in Indiana. My family moved to Florida when I was 4 years old. I had 1 sibling, a brother. My father was a barber so when the Florida season was over, we would spent every summer back in Indiana and he would barber there.

I was inspired to write after one of the worst thing in a mother's life happened. I lost my 26 year old son.

To survive this trauma, I had to get away, so my husband and I bought a small log cabin in northern Georgia. My husband remained in Florida to continue to run our business and my youngest son and I went to Georgia to get back to basics.

To escape my reality I read a book a day, I journaled and I wrote poetry.

I had read every book Sherryl Woods had written except for 2 that were out of print. I knew she had a bookstore in Florida so I called in search of these 2 books. To my surprise Sherryl answered the phone. She was so welcoming, so I told her how much her books had meant to me during a difficult time. They had allowed me to escape into the lives of the characters. She sent me the books, with a note in each one and her signature. She said I should give writing a try, so I started that night.

Small towns were where I felt the most at home. My family in Indiana were farmers and simple, basic people. I am still a small town girl.